The Story of Tracy Beaker

Tracy Beaker is by far the most popular of all the characters I've ever invented. How she would love to know that! She would just glory in the fact that there are now three books about her, a very popular long-running television series, a magazine, a musical, and all sorts of merchandising, from pyjamas to pencil cases!

Tracy's always been a very special character to me too, because *The Story of Tracy Beaker* was the first book of mine illustrated by Nick Sharratt. I knew I wanted to have lots of amusing black and white drawings within the text, as if Tracy had done them all herself whilst writing her own story. My editor said he knew the ideal illustrator and arranged for me to meet Nick at the publishers.

Nick and I greeted each other politely and made small talk, both of us feeling very shy. I liked Nick very much but my one worry was that he wasn't quite wild and wacky enough to draw like my totally weird Tracy. But then I bent down to get a hankie out of my handbag and spotted that Nick was wearing the most stingingly bright canary yellow socks – and I knew he'd be perfect! I've been so very lucky to be artistically partnered with Nick. I'm sure his brilliant inventive covers and expressive black and white illustrations are one of the main reasons why my books have been so successful.

The Story of Tracy Beaker has been the most successful. I got the idea from seeing photos of children in care in my local paper, all longing to be fostered. I looked at those touching pictures and wondered what it would be like to be advertised in that way. It would be great if you found brilliant foster parents as a result, but how would you feel if no-one at all came forward to meet up with you? I decided to write a story about a tough feisty little girl in a children's home who gets advertised like this.

I knew almost straight away that I was going to call her Tracy. It seemed a perfect modern street-wise bouncy sort of name. I had problems finding a suitable surname. I was thinking about it when I was lolling in my bath one morning. I peered all round the steamy room for some kind of inspiration. There aren't a lot of possibilities in the average bathroom! I wondered about Tracy Flannel, Tracy Soap, Tracy Tap, Tracy Toothbrush, Tracy Toilet – and decided I'd never ever find a sensible surname that way. I got on with washing my hair and then reached for the old plastic Snoopy beaker I kept on the side of the bath to rinse all the shampoo away. I stared at it. Tracy Beaker? Yes, I had the right name at last.

Jacqueline Wilson

BY JACQUELINE WILSON

ILLUSTRATED BY NICK SHARRATT

CORGI YEARLING BOOKS

THE STORY OF TRACY BEAKER
A CORGI YEARLING BOOK 978 0440 86757 9

First published in Great Britain by Doubleday,
an imprint of Random House Children's Publishers UK
A Random House Group Company

Doubleday edition published 1991
First Corgi Yearling edition published 1992
This Corgi Yearling edition published 2011

TRACY BEAKER'S THUMPING HEART

First published in Great Britain by Corgi Yearling,
an imprint of Random House Children's Publihers UK
A Random House Group Company

15 17 19 20 18 16 14

The Random House Group Limited supports The Forest Stewardship
Council® (FSC®), the leading international forest-certification organisation.
Our books carrying the FSC label are printed on FSC®-certified paper. FSC is
the only forest-certification scheme supported by the leading environmental
organisations, including Greenpeace. Our paper procurement policy can be
found at www.randomhouse.co.uk/environment

MIX
Paper from
responsible sources
FSC® C016897

Set in Century Schoolbook

Corgi Yearling Books are published by Random House Children's Publishers UK
61–63 Uxbridge Road, London W5 5SA

www.**randomhousechildrens**.co.uk
www.**randomhouse**.co.uk

Addresses for companies within The Random House Group Limited
can be found at: www.randomhouse.co.uk/offices.htm

THE RANDOM HOUSE GROUP Limited Reg. No. 954009

A CIP catalogue record for this book is available from the British Library.

Printed and bound by CPI Group (UK) Ltd, Croydon, CR0 4YY

To Bryony, David, Miranda,
Jason and Ryan

My name is   Tracy Beaker

I am 10 **years** 2 **months old**.

My birthday is on   8 May. It's not fair, because that dopey Peter Ingham has his birthday then too, so we just got the one cake between us. And we had to hold the knife to cut the cake together. Which meant we only had half a wish each. Wishing is for babies anyway. They don't come true.

I was born at   some hospital some-where. I looked cute when I was a little baby but I bet I yelled a lot.

I am   cms tall. I don't know. I've tried measuring with a ruler but it keeps wobbling about and I can't reach properly. I don't want to get any of the other children to help me. This is my private book.

I weigh   kgs. I don't know that either. Jenny has got scales in her bathroom but they're stones and pounds. I don't weigh many of them. I'm a little titch.

My eyes are black and I can make them go all wicked and witchy. I quite fancy being a witch. I'd make up all these incredibly evil spells and wave my wand and ZAP Louise's golden curls would all fall out and ZAP Peter Ingham's silly squeaky voice would get sillier and squeakier and he'd grow whiskers and a long tail and ZAP . . . there's not room on this bit of the page, but I've still got all sorts of ZAPs inside my head.

8

My hair is fair and very long and curly. I am telling fibs. It's dark and difficult and it sticks up in all the wrong places.

My skin is spotty when I eat a lot of sweets.

Stick a photo of yourself here

I'm not really cross-eyed. I was just pulling a silly face.

I started this book on   I don't know. Who cares what the date is? You always have to put the date at school. I got fed up with this and put 2091 in my Day Book and wrote about all these rockets and space ships and monsters legging it down from Mars to eat us all up, as if we'd all whizzed one hundred years into the future. Miss Brown didn't half get narked.

MORE THINGS ABOUT ME

Things I like

My lucky number is   7. So why didn't I get fostered by some fantastic rich family when I was seven then?

My favourite colour is   blood red, so watch out, ha-ha.

My best friend is Well, I've had heaps and heaps, but Louise has gone off with Justine and now I haven't got anyone just at the moment.

I like eating everything. I like birthday cake best. And any other kind of cake. And Smarties and Mars Bars and big buckets of popcorn and jelly spiders and Cornettos and Big Macs with French fries and strawberry milk shakes.

My favourite name is Camilla. There was a lovely little baby at this other home and that was her name. She was a really sweet kid with fantastic hair that I used to try to get into loads of little plaits and it must have hurt her sometimes but she never cried. She really liked me, little Camilla. She got fostered quick as a wink. I begged her foster mum and dad to bring her back to see me but they never did.

11

I like drinking pints of bitter. That's a joke. I *have* had a sip of lager once but I didn't like it.

My favourite game is playing with make-up. Louise and I once borrowed some from Adele who's got heaps. Louise was a bit boring and just tried to make herself look beautiful. I turned myself into an incredible vampire with evil shadowy eyes and blood dribbling down my chin. I didn't half scare the little ones.

My favourite animals is Well, there's a rabbit called Lettuce at this home but it's a bit limp, like its name. It doesn't sit up and give you a friendly lick like a dog. I think I'd like a Rottweiler – and then all my enemies had better WATCH OUT.

My favourite TV programme is horror films.

Bets of all I like being with my mum.

Things I don't like

the name Justine. Louise. Peter. Oh there's heaps and heaps of names I can't stand.

eating stew. Especially when it's got great fatty lumps in it. I used to have this horrid foster mother called Aunty Peggy and she was an awful cook. She used to make this slimy stew like molten sick and we were supposed to eat it all up, every single bit. Yuck.

Most of all I hate Justine. That Monster Gorilla. And not seeing my mum.

MY OWN FAMILY

Stick a photo of you and your family here

This was when I was a baby. See, I was sweet then. And this is my mum. She's ever so pretty. I wish I looked more like her.

The people in my own family are My mum. I don't have a dad. I lived with my mum when I was little and we got on great but then she got this Monster Gorilla Boyfriend and I hated him and he hated me back and beat me up and so I had to be taken into care. No wonder my mum sent him packing.

My own family live at I'm not sure exactly where my mum lives now because she has to keep moving about because she gets fed up living in one place for long.

The phone number is Well, I don't know, do I? Funny though, I always used to bag this toy telephone in the playhouse at school and pretend I was phoning my mum. I used to have these long long conversations with her. They were just pretend of course, but I was only about five then and sometimes it got to be quite real.

Things about my family that I like I like my mum because she's pretty and good fun and she brings me lovely presents.

MY FOSTER FAMILY

There's no point filling this bit in. I haven't got a foster family at the moment.

I've had two. There was Aunty Peggy and Uncle Sid first of all. I didn't like them much and I didn't get on with the other kids so I didn't care when they got rid of me. I was in a children's home for a while and then I had this other couple. Julie and Ted. They were young and friendly and they bought me a bike and I thought it was all going to be great and I went to live with them and I was ever so good and did everything they said and I thought I'd be staying with them until my mum came to get me for good but then . . . I don't want to write about it. It ended up with me getting turfed out THROUGH NO FAULT OF MY OWN. I was so mad I smashed up the bike so I don't even have that any more. And now I'm in a new children's home and they've advertised me in the papers but there weren't many takers and now I think they're getting a bit desperate. I don't care though. I expect my mum will come soon anyway.

MY SCHOOL

My school is called It's Kinglea Junior School. I've been to three other schools already. This one's OK I suppose.

My teacher is called Miss Brown. She gets cross if we just call her Miss.

Subjects I do Story-writing. Arithmetic. Games. Art. All sorts of things. And we do Projects only I never have the right stuff at the Home so I can't do it properly and get a star.

I like Story-writing best. I've written heaps of stories, and I do pictures for them too. I make some of them into books. I made Camilla a special baby book with big printed words and pictures of all the things she liked best, things like TEDDY and ICE CREAM and YOUR SPECIAL FRIEND TRACY.

I also like Art. We use poster paints. We've got them at the Home too but they get all gungy and mucked up and the brushes are useless. They've got good ones at school. This is a painting I did yesterday. If I was a teacher I'd give it a gold star. *Two* gold stars.

My class is   3a.

People in my class   I can't list all their names, I'd be here all night. I don't know some of them yet. There's not much point making friends because I expect I'll be moving on soon.

Other teachers   Oh, they're all boring. Who wants to write about them?

I get to school by   going in the Minibus. That's how all the kids in the home get to school. I'd sooner go in a proper car or walk it by myself but you're not allowed.

It takes   hours   mins
It varies. Sometimes it takes ages because the little kids can't find their pencil cases and the big ones try to bunk off and we just have to hang about waiting.

Things I don't like about school
They all wear grey things, that's the uniform, and I've only got navy things from my last school. The teachers know why and I don't get into trouble but the other kids stare.

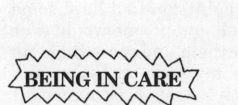

BEING IN CARE

My social worker is called Elaine and sometimes she's a right pain, ha-ha.

We talk about all sorts of boring things.

But I don't like talking about my mum. Not to Elaine. What I think about my mum is private.

IF I WAS . . .

older, I would live in this really great modern house all on my own, and I'd have my own huge bedroom with all my own things, special bunk beds just for me so that I'd always get the top one and a Mickey Mouse alarm clock like Justine's and my own giant set of poster paints and I'd have some felt tips as well and no-one would ever get to borrow them and mess them up and I'd have my own television and choose exactly what programmes I want, and I'd stay up till gone twelve every night and I'd eat at McDonald's every single day and I'd have a big fast car so I could whizz off and visit my mum whenever I wanted.

a policeman, I would arrest the Monster Gorilla and I'd lock him up in prison for ever.

a kitten, I would grow very long claws and sharp teeth and scratch and bite everyone so they'd get really scared of me and do everything I say.

yelled at, I would yell back.

invisible, I would spy on people.

very tall, I would stamp on people with my great big feet.

Very rich, I would buy my own house and then . . . I've done all that bit. I'm getting fed up writing all this. What's on the next page?

MY OWN STORY

Use this space to write your story

THE STORY OF TRACY BEAKER

Once upon a time there was a little girl called Tracy Beaker. That sounds a bit stupid, like the start of a soppy fairy story. I can't stand fairy stories. They're all the same. If you're very good and very beautiful with long golden curls then, after sweeping up a few cinders or having a long kip in a cobwebby palace, this prince comes along and you live happily ever after. Which is fine if you happen to be a goodie-goodie and look gorgeous. But if you're bad and ugly then you've got no chance whatsoever. You get given a silly name like *Rumpelstiltskin* and nobody invites you to their party and no-one's ever grateful even when you do them a whopping great favour. So of course you get a bit cheesed off with this sort of treatment. You stamp your feet in a rage and fall right through the floorboards or you scream yourself into a frenzy and you get locked up in a tower and they throw away the key.

I've done a bit of stamping and screaming in my time.

And I've been locked up heaps of times. Once they locked me up all day long. And all night. That was at the first Home, when I wouldn't settle because I wanted my mum so much. I was just little then but they still locked me up. I'm not fibbing. Although I do have a tendency to tell a few fibs now and again. It's funny, Aunty Peggy used to call it Telling Fairy Stories.

I'd say something like – 'Guess what, Aunty Peggy, I just met my mum in the back garden and she gave me a ride in her flash new sports car and we went down the shopping arcade and she bought me my very own huge bottle of scent, that posh *Poison* one, just like the bottle Uncle Sid gave you for your birthday, and I was messing about with it, playing Murderers, and the bottle sort of tipped and it's gone all over me as I expect you've noticed, but it's my scent not yours. I don't know what's happened to yours. I think one of the other kids took it.'

You know the sort of thing. I'd make it dead convincing but Aunty Peggy wouldn't even listen properly. She'd just shake her head at me and get all cross and red and say, 'Oh Tracy, you naughty girl, you're Telling Fairy Stories again.' Then she'd give me a smack.

Foster mothers aren't supposed to smack you at all. I told Elaine that Aunty Peggy used to smack me and Elaine sighed and said, 'Well sometimes, Tracy, you really do ask for it.' Which is a lie in itself. I have never in my life said 'Aunty Peggy, please will you give me a great big smack.' And her smacks really hurt too, right on the back of your leg where it stings most. I didn't like that Aunty Peggy at all. If I was in a real fairy story I'd put a curse on her. A huge wart right on the end of her nose? Frogs and toads coming wriggling out of her mouth every time she tries to speak? No, I can make up better than that. She can have permanent huge great bogeys hanging out of her nose that won't go away no matter how many times she blows it, and whenever she tries to speak she'll make this terribly loud Rude Noise. Great!

Oh dear. You can't win. Elaine, my stupid old social worker, was sitting beside me when I started writing THE STORY OF TRACY BEAKER and I got the giggles making up my brilliant curses for Aunty Peggy and Elaine looked surprised and said, 'What are you laughing at, Tracy?'

I said, 'Mind your own business' and she said, 'Now Tracy' and then she looked at what I'd written which is a bit of a cheek seeing as it's supposed to be very private. She sighed when she got to the Aunty Peggy part and said, 'Really Tracy!' and I said, 'Yes, really, Elaine.' And she sighed again and her lips moved for a moment or two. That's her taking a deep breath and counting up to ten. Social workers are supposed to do that when a child is being difficult. Elaine ends up doing an awful lot of counting when she's with me.

When she got to ten she gave me this big false smile. Like this.

'Now look, Tracy,' said Elaine. 'This is your own special book about you, something that you're going to keep for ever. You don't want to spoil it by writing all sorts of silly cheeky rude things in it, do you?'

I said, 'It's my life and it hasn't been very special so far, has it, so why shouldn't I write any old rubbish?'

Then she sighed again, but sympathetically this time, and she put her arm round me and said, 'Hey, I know you've had a hard time, but *you're* very special. You know that, don't you?'

I shook my head and tried to wriggle away.

'Yes, you are, Tracy. Very very special,' Elaine said, hanging on to me.

'Then if I'm so very very special how come no-one wants me?' I said.

'Oh dear, I know it must have been very disappointing for you when your second placement went wrong, love, but you mustn't let it depress you too much. Sooner or later you'll find the perfect placement.'

'A fantastic rich family?'

'Maybe a family. Or maybe a single person, if someone really suitable came along.'

I gave her this long look. 'You're single, Elaine. And I bet you're suitable. So why don't you foster me, eh?'

It was her turn to wriggle then.

'Well, Tracy. You know how it is. I mean, I've got my job. I have to deal with lots of children.'

'But if you fostered me you could stop bothering with all the others and just look after me. They give you money if you foster. I bet they'd give you lots extra because I'm difficult, and I've got behaviour problems and all that. How about it, Elaine? It would be fun, honest it would.'

'I'm sure it would be lots of fun, Tracy, but I'm sorry, it's just not on,' Elaine said.

She tried to give me a big hug but I pushed her hard.

'I was only joking,' I said. 'Yuck. I couldn't stand the thought of living with you. You're stupid and boring and you're all fat and wobbly, I'd absolutely hate the idea of you being my foster mum.'

'I can understand why you're angry with me, Tracy,' said Elaine, trying to look cool and calm, but sucking in her stomach all the same.

I told her I wasn't a bit angry, though I shouted as I said it. I told her I didn't care a bit, though I had these silly watery eyes. I didn't cry though. I don't *ever* cry. Sometimes people think I do, but it's my hay fever.

'I expect you're going to think up all sorts of revolting curses for me now,' said Elaine.

'I'm doing it right this minute,' I told her.

'OK,' she said.

'You always say OK,' I told her. 'You know: OK, that's fine with me, if that's what you want I'm not going to make a fuss; OK Tracy, yes I know you've got this socking great axe in your hand and you're about to chop off my head because you're feeling angry with me, but OK, if that's the way you feel, I'm not going to get worried about it because I'm this super-cool social worker.'

She burst out laughing then.

'No-one can stay super-cool when you're around, Tracy,' she said. 'Look kiddo, you write whatever you want in your life story. It's your own book, after all.'

So that's that. This is my own book and I can write whatever I want. Only I'm not quite sure what I do want, actually. Maybe Elaine *could* help after all. She's over the other side of the sitting-room, helping that wet Peter with his book. He hasn't got a clue. He's filling it all in *so* slowly and *so* seriously, not writing it but printing it with that silly blotchy biro of his, trying to do it ever so carefully but failing miserably, and now he's smudged some of it so it looks a mess anyway.

I've just called Elaine but she says she's got to help Peter for a bit. The poor little petal is getting all worried in case he puts the wrong answers, as if it's some dopey intelligence test. I've done heaps of them, intelligence tests. They're all ever so easy-peasy. I can do them quick as a wink. They always expect kids in care to be as thick as bricks, but I get a hundred out of a hundred nearly every time. Well, they don't tell you the answers, but I bet I do.

TRACY BEAKER IS A STUPID SHOW-OFF AND THIS IS THE SILLIEST LOAD OF RUBBISH I'VE EVER READ AND IF SHE'S SO SUPER-INTELLIGENT HOW COME SHE WETS HER BED LIKE A BABY ?

Ignore the stupid scribble up above. It's all lies anyway. It's typical. You can't leave anything for two minutes in this rotten place without one of the other kids spoiling it. But I never thought anyone would stoop so low as to write in my own private life story. And I know who did it too. I know, Justine Littlewood, and you just wait. I'm going to get you.

I went over to rescue Elaine from that boring wimpy little Peter and I had a little peer into his book and I nearly fell over, because you'll never guess who he's put as his best friend. Me. *Me!*

'Is this some sort of joke?' I demanded. He went all red and mumbly and tried to hide what he'd put, but I'd already seen it. *My best friend is Tracy Beaker*. It was down there on the page in black and white. Well, not your actual black and white, more your smudgy blue biro, but you know what I mean.

'Go away and stop pestering poor Peter,' Elaine said to me.

'Yes, but he's putting absolute rubbish in his book, Elaine, and it's stupid. I'm not Peter Ingham's best friend!'

'Well, I think it's very nice that Peter wants you to be his friend,' said Elaine. She pulled a funny face. 'There's no accounting for taste.'

'Oh, ha-ha. Why did you put that, Peter?'

Peter did a little squeak about sharing birthdays and so that made us friends.

'It does *not* make us friends, dumbo,' I declared.

Elaine started getting on at me then, saying I was being nasty to poor little Peetie-Weetie and if I couldn't be friendly why didn't I just push off and get on with my own life story? Well, when people tell me to push off I generally try to stick to them like glue, just to be annoying, so that's what I did.

And then, Jenny called me into the kitchen because she made out she wanted a hand getting the lunch ready, but that was just a *ploy*. Jenny doesn't smack. She doesn't even often tell you off. She just uses ploys and tries to distract you. It sometimes works with the thicker kids but it usually has no effect whatsoever on me. However, I quite like helping in the kitchen because you can generally nick a spoonful of jam or a handful of raisins when Jenny's back is turned. So I went along to the kitchen and helped her put an entire shoal of fish fingers under the double grill while she got the chip pan bubbling. Fish fingers don't taste so great when they're raw. I tried nibbling just to see. I don't know why they're called fish *fingers*. They don't have fingers, do they? They ought to be fish *fins*. That Aunty Peggy used to make this awful milk pudding called tapioca which had these little slimy bubbly bits and I told the other kids that they were fish eyes. And I told the really little ones that marmalade is made out of goldfish and they believed that too.

When Jenny started serving out the fish fingers and chips, I went back into the sitting-room to tell everyone that lunch was ready. And I remember seeing Louise and Justine hunched up in a corner, giggling over something they'd got hidden. I don't know. I *am* highly intelligent, I truly wasn't making that up, and yet it was a bit thick of me not to twig what they were up to. Which was reading my own life story and then scribbling all over it.

A little twit like Peter Ingham would tell, but I'm no tell-tale tit. I shall simply get my own back. I shall think long and carefully for a suitable horrible revenge. I don't half hate that Justine. Before she came Louise and I were best friends and we did everything together and, even though I was still dumped in a rotten children's home, it really wasn't so bad. Louise and I made out we were sisters and we had all these secrets and—

One of these secrets was about a certain small problem that I have. A night-time problem. I've got my own room and so it was always a private problem that only Jenny and I knew

34

about. Only to show Louise we were the bestest friends ever I told her about it. I knew it wasn't a sensible move right from the start because she giggled, and she used to tease me about it a bit even when we were still friends. And then she went off with Justine and I'd sometimes worry that she might tell on me, but I always convinced myself she'd never ever stoop that low. Not Louise.

But she has told. She's told Justine, my worst enemy. So what am I going to do to her? Any ideas ticking away inside my head?

Well, I could beat her up.

Tick, tick, tick.
I could deliver a karate chop death blow.

Tick, tick, tick.
I could get my mum to come in her car and
run her over, squashing her hedgehog-flat.

Tick, tick, tick. Hey! Tick tock. Tick tock. *I* know. And I also know I'm not leaving this book hanging about. From now on I shall carry it on my person. So, ha-ha, sucks boo to you, Justine Littlewood. Oh you're going to get it. Yes you are, yes you are, tee-hee.

I'm writing this at midnight. I can't put the light on because Jenny might still be prowling about and I don't want *another* ding-dong with her, thanks very much. I'm making do with a torch, only the battery's going, so there's just this dim little glow and I can hardly see what I'm doing. I wish I had something to eat. In all those Enid Blyton school stories they always have midnight feasts. The food sounds a bit weird, sardines and condensed milk, but I could murder a Mars Bar right this minute. Imagine a Mars Bar as big as this bed. Imagine licking it, gnawing away at a corner, scooping out the soft part with both fists. Imagine the wonderful chocolatey smell. I'm slavering at the thought. Yes, that's what those little marks are on the page. Slavers. I don't cry. I don't *ever* cry.

I acted as if I didn't care less when Jenny had a real go at me. And I don't.

'I think you really do care, Tracy,' she said, in that silly sorrowful voice. 'Deep down I think you're really very sorry.'

'That's just where you're wrong,' I insisted.

'Come off it now. You must know how you'd feel if your mother had bought you a special present and one of the other kids spoilt it.'

As she said that I couldn't help remembering being in the first Home, long before the dreaded Aunty Peggy or that mean hateful unfair Julie and Ted. My mum came to see me and she'd brought this doll, a doll almost as big as me, with long golden curls and a bright blue lacy dress to match her big blue eyes. I'd never liked dolls all that much but I thought this one was wonderful. I called her Bluebell and I undressed her right down to her frilly white knickers and dressed her up again and brushed her blonde curls and made her blink her big blue eyes, and at night she'd lie in my bed and we'd have these cosy little chats and she'd tell me that Mum was coming back really soon, probably tomorrow, and—

OK, that sort of thing makes me want to puke now but I was only little then and I didn't know any better. The housemother let me cart Bluebell all over the place but she tried to make me give the other kids a go at playing with her. Well, I wasn't going to let that lot maul her about, so of course I didn't let them hold her. But I came unstuck when I started school. You weren't allowed to take toys to school, only on Friday afternoons. I cried and fought but they wouldn't let me. So I had to start leaving Bluebell at home. I'd tuck her up in my bed with her eyes closed, pretending she was asleep, and then when I got home from school I'd charge upstairs into our crummy little dormitory and wake her up with a big hug. Only one day I woke her up and I got the shock of my life. Her eyelids snapped open but her blue eyes had vanished inside her head. Some rotten lousy pig had given them a good poke. I couldn't stand it, seeing those creepy empty sockets. She stopped being my friend. She just scared me.

The housemother took Bluebell off to this dolls' hospital and they gave her some new eyes. They were blue too, but not the same bright blue, and they didn't blink properly either. They either got stuck altogether or they flashed up and down all the time, making her look silly and fluttery. But I didn't really care then. She was spoilt. She wasn't the same Bluebell. She didn't talk to me any more.

I never found out which kid had done it. The housemother said it was A Mystery. Just One Of Those Things.

Jenny didn't call it a mystery when Justine

went sobbing to her because her silly old Mickey Mouse alarm clock had got broken. Clocks break all the time. It's not as if it's a really flash expensive clock. If I'd been Jenny I'd have told Justine to stop making such a silly fuss. I'd have stopped up my ears when that sneaky little twerp started going on about me. 'I bet I know who did it too, Jenny. *That Tracy Beaker.*'

Yes, she sneaked on me. And Jenny listened, because she came looking for me. She had to look quite a long time. I kind of suspected what was coming, so I cleared off. I didn't try to hide in the house or the garden like one of the little kids. I'm not that dumb. They can flush you out in five minutes no matter where you are. No, I skipped it out the back door and down the road and went for a wander round the town.

It was great. Yes, I had the most amazing time. First I went to McDonald's and had a Big Mac and French fries with a strawberry milk

shake and then I went to the pictures and saw this really funny film and I laughed so much I fell out of my seat and then I went off with this whole crowd of friends to an amusement arcade and I kept winning the jackpot on the fruit machines and then we all went off to this party and I drank a whole bottle of wine and it was great, it just tasted like lemonade, and this girl there, we made friends and she asked me if I'd like to stay the night, sharing her twin beds in this fantastic pink and white room, in fact she said I could stay there permanently if I really wanted and so I said . . .

I said: 'No thanks, I'd sooner go back to my crummy children's home.'?

Of course I didn't say that. Well, she didn't say it either. I sort of made her up. And her party. I didn't go down the amusement arcade. Or to the pictures. Or McDonald's. I *would* have done, but I couldn't, on account of the fact I ran off with no cash whatsoever.

I said I tell fibs sometimes. It makes things more interesting. I mean, what's the point of writing what I really did? Which was loaf about the town feeling more and more fed up. The only thing I could think of to do was sit in the bus shelter. It got a bit boring. I pretended I was waiting for a bus and I tried to think of all the places I'd like to go to. But that began to depress me because I started thinking about Watford, where my mum said she lived. And last year I got all the right money together (which created a few problems afterwards as I sort of borrowed it without asking) and sussed out the journey and got all these trains and buses and all the rest of it, so that I could pay my mum a visit and give her a lovely surprise. Only it was me that got the surprise because she wasn't there, and the people who lived in that house said she'd moved on about six months ago and they didn't have a clue where she'd gone now.

So it's going to take a bit of organized searching to find her again. I could catch a different bus every day for the rest of my life and maybe not find her. It's hard when you haven't got a clue where to look.

I was still scrunched up in the bus shelter when a familiar white Minivan hoved into view. It was Mike, come looking for me. Mike looks after us with Jenny. He isn't half a bore. He doesn't often get cross but he whinges on about Rules and Responsibility and a whole lot of other rubbish.

So by the time I'd got back to the Home I was sick to death of the subject, but then Jenny came into my bedroom and *she* started. And she

assumed it was me that broke Justine's clock though she had no proof whatsoever. I told her so, and said she just liked picking on me, and it wasn't fair. She said I'd feel better if I owned up to breaking Justine's clock and then went to say sorry to her. I said she had to be joking. I wasn't the slightest bit sorry and anyway I didn't didn't *didn't* break Justine's rotten clock.

That isn't necessarily a fib. I don't absolutely one hundred percent *know* that I broke it. All right, I did go into her bedroom when she was in the bathroom, and I did pick up the clock to look at it. Well, she's always going on about it because she's got this boring thing about her dad. She makes out he's so flipping special when he hardly ever comes to see her. The only thing he's ever given her is that stupid tinny old alarm clock. I wanted to look at it to see if it was really so special. Well, it wasn't. I bet he just got it from Woolworth's. And it certainly wasn't made very carefully because when I twiddled the knobs to make the little Mickey on the end of the hands go whizzing round and round he couldn't keep it up for very long. There was this sudden whir and clunk and then the hand fell off altogether and Mickey fell too, with his little paws in the air, dead.

But he might have been about to take his last gasp anyway. That hand might well have fallen off the next time Justine touched the stupid clock to wind it up.

I'm not going to say sorry no matter what.

I wish I could get to sleep.

I'll try counting sheep . . .

I *still* can't get to sleep and it's the middle of the night now and it's rotten and I keep thinking about my mum. I wish she'd come and get me. I wish anyone would come and get me. Why can't I ever get a good foster family? That Aunty Peggy and Uncle Sid were lousy. But then I could suss them out and tell they were lousy right from the start. Anyone who smacks hard and serves up frogspawn for your pudding is certainly not an ideal aunty. But last time, when I got fostered by Julie and Ted, I really thought it was all going to work out happily ever after, and that it was my turn to be the golden princess instead of a *Rumpelstiltskin*.

They were great at first, Julie and Ted. That's what I called them right from the start. They didn't want to be a prissy aunty and uncle. And Julie said she didn't want me to call her Mum because I already had a mum. I thought such a lot of Julie when she said that. She wasn't exactly my idea of a glamorous foster mum – she had this long wispy brown hair and she wore sludge-coloured smocky things and sandals – and Ted looked a bit of a wimp too with his glasses and his beard and weirdo comfy walking shoes, not so much Hush Puppy as Shut-your-face Hound-Dog – but I thought they were the sort of couple you could really trust. Ha!

Because I went to live with them and I thought we were getting on really great, though they were a bit boringly strict about stuff like sweets and bedtimes and horror videos, but then Julie started to wear bigger smocks than ever and lolled about on the sofa and Ted got all misty-eyed behind his glasses and I started to realize that something was up. And so I asked them what it was and they hedged and pulled faces at each other and then they looked shifty and told me that everything was fine and I knew they were lying. Things weren't fine at all.

They didn't even have the guts to tell me themselves. They left it to Elaine. She'd only just started to be my social worker then (I've had heaps because they kept moving around and leaving me behind and I got passed on like a parcel). I wasn't that keen on Elaine in those days. In fact I was really narked with her, because I'd had this man social worker Terry before her and he used to call me Smartie and he used to give me the odd tube of Smarties too, and I felt Elaine was a very poor substitute.

I wish I hadn't thought of those Smarties. I wish I had some now, I'm simply starving.

I'm sure Elaine marked me down as Sulky and Non-co-operative in her little notebook. The day she told me the Julie and Ted Bombshell I'm sure she scribbled TRACY TOTALLY GOB-SMACKED. Because Julie was having her own baby, after years of thinking she couldn't have any kids.

I didn't get it at first.

'So what's the problem, Elaine?' I said. 'We'll be a proper family then, four of us instead of three.'

Elaine was having difficulties finding the right words. She kept opening her mouth and closing it again, not saying a sausage.

'You look just like a fish when you do that, did you know?' I said cheekily, because my heart was starting to hammer hard against my chest and I knew that when Elaine eventually got the words out I wouldn't like the sound of them.

'The thing is, Tracy . . . Well, Julie and Ted have loved fostering you, and they've got very fond of you, but . . . you see, now they're having their own baby they feel that they're not really going to be able to cope.'

'Oh, I get it,' I said, in this jokey silly voice. 'So they're going to give the boring old baby away because they can't cope with it. And keep me. Because they had me first, didn't they?'

'Tracy—'

'They're not really going to dump me, are they?'

'They still very much want to keep in touch with you and—'

'So why can't I go on living with them? Look, I'll help all I can. Julie doesn't need to worry. I'll be just like a second mum to this baby. I know all what to do. I can give it its bottle and change its soggy old nappy and thump it on its back to bring up its wind. I'm dead experienced where babies are concerned.'

'Yes, I know, Tracy. But that's the trouble. You see, when Julie and Ted first fostered you, we did tell them a bit about your background, and the trouble you had in your first foster home. You know, when you shut the baby up in the cupboard—'

'That was Steve. And he wasn't a baby. He was a foul little toddler, and he kept mucking up our bedroom so I tidied him up into the cupboard just for a bit so I could get everything straightened out.'

'And there was the ghost game that got totally out of hand—'

'Oh that! All those little kids *loved* that game. I was ever so good at finding the right hiding places and then I'd start an eerie sort of moan and then I'd jump out at them, wearing this old white sheet.'

49

'And everyone got scared silly.'

'No they didn't. They just squealed because they were excited. *I* was the one who should have been scared, because they were all the ghost-busters you see, and I was the poor little ghost and—'

'OK, OK, but the point is, Tracy, it makes it plain in your records that you don't always get on well with little children.'

'That's a whopping great lie! What about Camilla? I looked after her at that children's home and she loved me, she really did.'

'Yes, I'm sure that's true, Tracy, but— Well, the thing is, Julie and Ted still feel they don't want to take any chances. They're worried you might feel a bit uncomfortable with a baby in the house.'

'So they're pushing me out?'

'But like I said, they still want to keep in touch with you and maybe take you out for tea sometimes.'

'No way,' I said. 'I don't want to see them ever again.'

'Oh Tracy, that's silly. That's just cutting off your own nose to spite your face,' said Elaine.

That's such a daft expression. How on earth would you go about it?

It wouldn't half hurt.

It hurt a lot leaving Julie and Ted's.

They wanted me to stay for a few months but I couldn't clear out of there quick enough. So here I am in this dump. They've tried to see me twice but I wasn't having any of it. I don't want any visitors, thanks very much. Apart from my mum. I wonder where she is. And why didn't she leave a forwarding address at that last place? And how will she ever get to find me here? Yeah, that's the problem. I bet she's been trying and trying to get hold of me, but she doesn't know where to look. Last time I saw her I was at Aunty Peggy's. I bet Mum's been round to Aunty Peggy's and I bet that silly old smacking-machine wouldn't tell her where I'd gone. So I bet my mum got really mad with her. And if she found out just how many times that Aunty Peggy smacked me then wow, ker-pow, splat, bang, I bet my mum would really let her have it.

I don't half want my mum.

I know why I can't sleep. It's because I'm so starving hungry, that's why. Crying always makes me hungry. Not that I've been crying now. I don't *ever* cry.

I think maybe I'll try slipping down to the kitchen. Jenny's bound to be fast asleep by now. Yeah, that's what I'll do.

I'm back. I've had my very own midnight feast. And it was absolutely delicious too. Well, it wasn't bad. I couldn't find any chocolate, of course, and that was what I really fancied. But I found an opened packet of cornflakes and got stuck into them, and then I tried raiding the fridge. There weren't too many goodies. I didn't go a bundle on tomorrow's uncooked mince or yesterday's cold custard, but I poked my finger in the butter and then dabbled it in the sugar bowl and that tasted fine. I did quite a lot of poking and dabbling actually. I know Jenny might notice so I got my little finger nail and drew these weeny lines like teethmarks and then did some paw prints all over the butter, so she'd think it was a mouse. Mice do eat butter, don't they? They like cheese, which is the same sort of thing. Of course this is going to have to be a mountaineering mouse, armed with ice-pick

and climbing boots, able to trek up the grim north face of the Frigidaire. And then it's got to develop Mighty Mouse muscles to prise open the door of the fridge to get at the feast inside.

Maybe Jenny will still be a teensy bit suspicious. But I can't help that. At least she didn't catch me while I was noshing away at my midnight feast.

Someone else did though. Not in the kitchen. Afterwards, when I was sneaking up the stairs again. They're very dark, these stairs, and they take a bit of careful negotiating. One of the little kids is quite likely to leave a teddy or a rattle or a building brick halfway up and you can come an awful cropper and wake the entire household. So I was feeling my way very very cautiously when I heard this weird little moaning sound coming from up on the landing. So I looked up, sharpish, and I could just make out this pale little figure, all white and trailing, and it was so exactly like a ghost that I opened my mouth to scream.

But Tracy Beaker has a lot of bottle. I'm not scared of anybody. Not even ghosts. So I clapped my hand over my mouth to stop the scream and pattered right on up the stairs to confront this puny little piece of ectoplasm. Only it wasn't a ghost after all. It was just snivelling drivelling Peter Ingham, clutching some sheets.

'Whatever are you up to, creep?' I whispered.

'Nothing,' Peter whispered back.

'Oh sure. You just thought you'd take your sheets for a walk in the middle of the night,' I said.

Peter flinched away from me.

'You've wet them haven't you?' I said.

'No,' Peter mumbled. He's a useless liar.

'Of course you've wet them. And you've been trying to wash them out in the bathroom, I know. So that people won't guess.'

'Oh don't tell, Tracy, please,' Peter begged.

'What do you take me for? I'm no tell-tale,' I said. 'And look, you don't have to fuss. Just get Jenny on her own in the morning and whisper to her. She'll sort it all out for you. She doesn't get cross.'

'Really?'

'Truly. And what you do now, you get yourself some dry sheets from the airing cupboard, right? And some pyjamas. Goodness, you don't know anything, do you? How long have you been in care?'

'Three months, one week, two days,' said Peter.

'Is that all? I've been in and out of care nearly all my life,' I said, getting the sheets for him. 'So why are you here now then? Your mum and dad get fed up with you? Can't say as I blame them.'

'They died when I was little. So I lived with my nan. But then she got old and then – then she died too,' Peter mumbled. 'And I didn't have anyone else so I had to come here. And I don't like it.'

'Well, of course you don't like it. But this is a lot better than most children's homes. You ought to have tried some of the places I've been in. They lock you up and they beat you and they practically starve you to death and then when they do give you meals it's absolutely disgusting, they pretend it's meat but it's really chopped up worms and dried dog's muck and—'

'Shut up Tracy,' Peter said, holding his stomach.

'Who are you telling to shut up?' I said, but not really fiercely. 'Go on, you'd better shove off back to your room. And put your dry pyjamas on. You're shivering.'

'OK, Tracy. Thanks.' He paused, fidgeting and fumbling with his sheets. 'I wish you would be my friend, Tracy.'

'I don't really bother making friends,' I said. 'There's not much point, because my mum's probably coming to get me soon and then I'll be living with her so I won't need any friends here.'

'Oh,' said Peter, and he sounded really disappointed.

'Still. I suppose you can be my friend just for now,' I said.

I don't know why I said it. Who wants to be lumbered with a silly little creep like that? I'm too kind-hearted, that's my trouble.

There wasn't much point in getting to sleep, because when I did eventually nod off I just had these stupid nightmares. It's as if there's a video inside my head and it switches itself on the minute my eyes close and I keep hoping it's going to be showing this great comedy that'll have me in stitches but then the creepy music starts and I know I'm in for it. Last night was the Great Horror Movie of all time. I was stuck in the dark somewhere and there was something really scary coming up quick behind me so I had to run like mad. Then I got to this big round pool

and there were these stepping stones with
people perching on them and I jumped on to the
first one and there was no room at all because
that fat Aunty Peggy was spread all over it. I
tried to cling to her but she gave me a big smack
and sent me flying. So then I jumped on to the
next stepping stone and Julie and Ted were
there and I tried to grab hold of them but they
just turned their backs on me and didn't even
try to catch me when I fell and so I had to try to
reach the next stepping stone but I was in the
water doing my doggy-paddle and it was getting

harder and harder, and every time I swam to a stepping stone all these people prodded at me with sticks and pushed me away and I kept going under the water and . . .

. . . and then I woke up and I know that whenever I dream about water it spells Trouble with a capital T. I had to make my own dash to the airing cupboard and the laundry basket. I was unfortunate enough to bump into Justine too. She didn't look as if she'd slept much either. He eyes seemed a bit on the red side. I couldn't help feeling a bit mean then, in spite of everything. So I gave her this big smile and I said, 'I'm sorry about what happened to your alarm clock, Justine.'

I didn't exactly tell her that *I* did it. Because I still don't know that it really was me. And anyway, I'd be a fool to admit it, wouldn't I? But I told her that I was still sorry, just like Jenny had suggested.

Only there's no point trying to be nice to pigs like Justine Littlewood. She didn't smile back and graciously accept my apologies.

'You'll be even sorrier when I've finished with you, Tracy Beaker,' she hissed. 'And what have you been doing, eh? Wet the bed again? Baby!' She hissed a lot more too. Stupid insulting things. I'm not going to waste any time writing them all down. Words can't hurt me anyway. Only I can't help being just a bit worried about that threat. What's she going to do to get her own back for the clock? If only we had poxy locks on our bedroom doors. Still, at least we've got separate bedrooms in this Home, even though they're weeny like cupboards.

It's new policy. Children in care need their own space. And I want to stay in my own space, doing all this writing, but Jenny has just put her head round my door and told me to buzz out into the garden with the others. And I said No Fear. Being in a Home is lousy at the best of times, but I just can't stick it in the school holidays when you're all cooped up together and the big ones bully you and the little ones pester you and the ones your own age gang up on you and have secrets together and call you names.

'Hows about trying to make it up with Justine?' Jenny suggested, coming to sit on my bed.

So I snorted and told her she was wasting her time, and more to the point, she was wasting *my* time, because I wanted to get on with my writing.

'You've done ever such a lot, Tracy,' said Jenny, looking at all these pages. 'We'll be running out of paper soon.'

'Then I'll use the backs of birthday cards. Or bog roll. Anything. I'm inspired, see. I can't stop.'

'Yes, you've really taken to this writing. Going to be a writer when you grow up, eh?'

'Maybe.' I hadn't thought about it before. I was always sure I was going to be on telly with my own chat show. THE TRACY BEAKER EXPERIENCE and I'd walk out on to this stage in a sparkly dress and all the studio audience would clap and cheer and all these really famous celebrities would fight tooth and nail to get on my show to speak to me. But I reckon I could write books too.

'Tell you what, Tracy. We've got a real writer coming round some time this afternoon. You could ask her for a few tips.'

'What's she coming for?'

'Oh, she's doing this article for a magazine about children in care.'

'Oh that boring old stuff,' I said, pretending to yawn but inside I start fizzing away.

I wouldn't mind my story being written up in some magazine. A book would be better of course, but maybe that could come later. I'd have to be careful what she said about me though. Elaine the Pain made a right mess of my newspaper advert. I was Child of the Week in the local paper. If she'd only let me write it I'd have been bowled over by people rushing to adopt dear little Tracy Beaker. I know just how to present myself in the right sort of way.

TRACY BEAKER

HAVE YOU A PLACE IN YOUR HEARTS FOR DEAR LITTLE TRACY? BRILLIANT AND BEAUTIFUL, THIS LITTLE GIRL NEEDS A LOVING HOME. VERY RICH PARENTS PREFERRED, AS LITTLE TRACY NEEDS LOTS OF TOYS, PRESENTS AND PETS TO MAKE UP FOR HER TRAGIC PAST.

Elaine is useless. Doesn't have a clue. She didn't even let me get specially kitted out for the photograph.

'We want you looking natural, Tracy,' she said.

Well I turned out looking too flipping natural. Hair all over the place and a scowl on my face because that stupid photographer kept treating me like a baby, telling me to Watch the Birdie. And the things Elaine wrote about me!

TRACY

Tracy is a lively, healthy, chatty, ten-year-old who has been in care for a number of years. Consequently she has a few behaviour problems and needs firm, loving handling in a long-term foster home.

I ask you!

'How could you *do* this to me, Elaine?' I shrieked when I saw it. 'Is that the best thing you can say about me? That I'm *healthy*? And anyway I'm not. What about my hay fever?'

'I also say you're lively. And chatty.'

'Yeah. Well, we all know what that means. Cheeky. Difficult. Bossy.'

'You said it, Tracy,' Elaine murmured.

'And all this guff about behaviour problems! What do I do, eh? I don't go round beating people up? Well, not many. And I don't smash the furniture. Hardly ever.'

'Tracy, it's very understandable that you have a few problems—'

'I *don't*! And then how could you ask for someone to handle me *firmly*?'

'And lovingly,' said Elaine. 'I put loving too.'

'Oh yes, they'll tell me how much they love me as they lay into me with a cane. Honestly, Elaine, you're round the twist. You're just going to attract a bunch of creepy child-beaters with this crummy advert.'

But it didn't even attract them. No-one replied at all.

Elaine kept telling me not to worry, as if it was somehow my fault. I know if she'd only get her act together and do a really flash advert there'd be heaps of offers. I bet.

But maybe I'm wasting my time nagging Elaine. This woman who's coming this afternoon might be just the chance I've been waiting for. If she's a real writer then she'll know how to jazz it all up so that I sound really fantastic. Only I've got to present myself to her in a special way so that she'll pick me out from all the others and just do a feature on me. So what am I going to do, eh?

Aha!

Not aha. More like boo-hoo. Only I don't ever cry, of course.

I don't want to write down what happened. I don't think I want to be a writer any more.

I tried, I really did. I went flying up to my bedroom straight after lunch and I did my best to make myself look pretty. I know my hair is untidy so I tried scragging it back into these little sticky-out plaits. Camilla had little plaits and everyone cooed over them and said how cute she looked. I thought my face looked a bit bare when I'd done the plaits so I wetted some of the side bits with spit and tried to make them go into curls.

I still looked a bit boring so I decided to liven my face up a bit. So I sneaked round to Adele's room. She's sixteen and she's got a Saturday job in BHS and she's got a drawer absolutely chock-a-block with make-up. I borrowed a bit of blusher to give myself some colour in my cheeks. And then I thought I'd try out a pink glossy lipstick too. And mascara to make my eyelashes look long. I tried a bit on my eyebrows too, to

make them stand out. And I put a lot of powder on to be like the icing on a cake. I thought I looked OK when I'd finished. Well, at least I looked different.

I changed my clothes too. I didn't want this writer to see me in a scrubby old T-shirt and skirt. No way. It had to be posh frock time. Only I don't really have a posh frock of my own. I did try on a few of Adele's things but somehow they didn't really suit me.

So then I started thinking about all the other girls. Louise had this really fantastic frock that she got a couple of years ago from some auntie. A real posh party frock with smocking and a flouncy skirt and its own sewn-in frilly white petticoat. It was a bit small for her now, of course, but she could just about squeeze into it for special days. And Louise and I are about the same size.

I knew Louise would go spare if she saw me parading around in her best party frock but I decided it might be worth it if I made a great impression on the writer woman first. So I beetled along the corridor towards her room, but I didn't have any luck. Louise was in her room. With Justine. I heard their voices.

They were discussing me, actually. And nappies. They were snorting with laughter and normally I'd have marched right in and punched their silly smirky faces but I knew if I got into a fight Jenny would send me to my room and make me stay there and I'd miss out on meeting the woman writer.

So with *extreme* self-control I walked away, still musing on what I was going to wear. I know it's summer, but I'd started to feel a bit shaky and shivery so I put on this mohair sweater that Julie knitted me for Christmas. When Julie and Ted dumped me I vowed not to have anything to do with them and I even thought about cutting up the mohair sweater into little woolly hankies but I couldn't quite do it. It's a pretty fantastic sweater actually, with the name Tracy in bright blue letters. That way it's obvious it's mine, specially made for me. Of course it's a bit tickly and prickly, but my mum once said you have to suffer if you want to look beautiful.

She's always looked beautiful. I don't half wish I took after her. I wasn't too bad as a baby. I was still quite cute as a toddler. But then I went off in a big way.

Still, I was trying my hardest to look OK. I only had my old skirt to wear with my mohair sweater, and there were dark blue stains all down one side where a biro exploded in my pocket, but I couldn't help that. The woman writer might just think it was a tie-and-dye effect. And at least the blue matched the lettering on my jumper.

I kept on prinking and preening in my room. I heard all the other kids go clattering downstairs. I heard Louise and Justine go giggle-snigger-titter along the corridor. My face started burning so that I didn't need my blusher. Then I heard Adele rampaging around because some rotten so-and-so had been in her room and rifled through all her make-up and mucked it all up. I decided to hang about in my room a bit longer.

I heard the front door bell. I heard Jenny talking to someone down in the hall. I heard them go into the sitting-room. I knew it was time to make my Entrance.

So I went running down the stairs and barging into the sitting-room with this great big smile on my face. It's no use looking sad or sulky if you want people to like you. Mum always tells me to give her a big smile. Even when she's saying goodbye to me. You can't look gloomy or it just upsets people and they don't want any more to do with you.

You've got to have this great big s-s-s-m-m-m-i-i-i-l-l-l-e-e-e.

68

Everyone looked up at me when I went into the sitting-room. And they all smiled too. Just for a moment I was daft enough to think they were all smiling back at me. But then I saw they were the wrong sort of smiles. They were smirks. And Justine and Louise nudged each other and giggled and spluttered and whooped. And Adele glared at me. Peter Ingham was the only one with a proper smile. He came over to me. He was blinking a bit rapidly.

'You look . . . nice, Tracy,' he said.

But I knew he was lying. It was no use kidding myself. It was obvious I looked a right prat. Jenny's pretty laid back about appearances but even she looked shocked at the sight of me. And it looked like all that effort was for nothing, because she didn't seem to have the woman writer person with her after all.

I've seen women writers on chat shows on the telly. They're quite glamorous, like film stars, with glittery frocks and high heels and lots of jewellery. They look a bit like my mum, only nowhere near as pretty of course.

The woman with Jenny looked like some boring social worker or teacher. Scruffy brown hair. No make-up. Scrubby T-shirt and rumpled jeans. A bit like me on an off-day, grown up.

69

I decided to slope off back to my bedroom. It seemed sensible to steer clear of Adele anyway. But Jenny caught hold of me by the back of my jumper.

'Hang about, Tracy. I thought you wanted to meet Cam Lawson.'

'Who?' I said.

'You know. The writer. I told you,' Jenny hissed. Then she lowered her voice even more. 'Why are you wearing your winter jumper when it's boiling hot today? And what on earth have you done to your face?'

'She thinks she looks pretty,' said Justine, and she clutched Louise and they both shrieked.

'Pipe down, you two,' said Jenny. 'Tracy. Tracy!' She hung on to me firmly, stopping me barging over to that stupid pair of titterers so as I could bang their heads together. 'Leave them, Tracy. Come and meet Cam.'

I wanted to meet this Cam (what sort of a silly name is that?) even though she didn't look a bit like a *proper* writer, but I sort of hung back. I'm usually the last person to feel shy, but somehow I suddenly didn't know what to say or what to do. So I growled something at Jenny and twisted away from her and stood in a corner by myself, just watching.

Peter came trotting after me. Justine and

Louise were still having hysterics at my appearance. You could tell they'd actually got over the giggles by this time, but Justine kept going into further false whoops and Louise was almost as bad.

'Don't take any notice of them,' Peter whispered.

'I don't,' I said crossly.

'I like your jumper,' said Peter. 'And your make-up. And the new hairstyle.'

'Then you're mad. It looks a mess. I look a mess. I look a mess *on purpose*,' I said fiercely. 'So you needn't feel sorry for me, Peter Ingham. You just clear off and leave me alone, right?'

Peter fidgeted from one foot to the other, looking worried.

'Clear off, you stupid little creep,' I said.

So of course he did clear off then. I wondered why I'd said it. OK, he *is* a creep, but he's not really that bad. I'd said he could be my friend. And it was a lot better when he was with me than standing all by myself, watching everyone over the other side of the room clustered round this Cam person calling herself a writer.

She's a weird sort of woman if you ask me. She was chatting away and yet you could tell she was really nervous inside. She kept fidgeting

with her pen and notebook and I was amazed to see she bites her nails! She's a great big grown-up woman and yet she does a dopey kid's thing like that. Well, she's not great big, she's little and skinny, but even so!

My mum has the most beautiful fingernails, very long and pointy and polished. She varnishes them every day. I just love that smell of nail varnish, that sharp peardrop niff that makes your nostrils twitch. Jenny caught me happily sniffing nail varnish one day, and do you know what she thought? Only that I was inhaling it, like glue sniffing. Did you ever? I let her think it too. *I* wasn't going to tell her I just liked the smell because it reminds me of Mum.

I'll tell you another weird thing about Cam Whatsit. She sat on one of our rickety old chairs, her legs all draped round the rungs, and she talked *to* the children. Most adults that come here talk *at* children.

They tell you what to do.

They go on and on about themselves.

They talk about you.

They ask endless stupid questions.

They make personal comments.

Even the social workers are at it. Or they strike this special nothing-you-can-say-would-shock-me-sweetie pose and they make stupid statements.

'I guess you're feeling really angry and upset today, Tracy,' they twitter, when I've wrecked my bedroom or got into a fight or shouted and sworn at someone, so that it's *obvious* I'm angry and upset.

They do this to show me that they understand. Only they don't understand peanuts. *They're* not the ones in care. I am.

I thought Cam Thing would ask questions and take down case histories in her notebook, all brisk and organized. But from what I could make out over in the corner she had a very different way of doing things.

She smiled a bit and fidgeted a lot and sort of weighed everybody up, and they all had a good stare at her. Two of the little kids tried to climb up on to her lap because they do that to anyone who sits down. It's not because they *like* the person, it's just they like being cuddled. They'd cry to have a cuddle with a cross-eyed gorilla, I'm telling you.

Most strangers to children's homes get all flattered and make a great fuss of the littlies and come on like Mary Poppins. This Cam seemed a bit surprised, even a bit put out. I don't blame her. Little Wayne in particular has got the runniest nose of all time and he likes to bury his head affectionately into your chest, wiping it all down your front.

Cam held him at arm's length, and when he tried his burrowing trick she distracted him by giving him her pen. He liked flicking the catch up and down.

She let little Becky have a ride on her foot at the same time, so she didn't feel left out and bawl. Becky kept trying to climb up her leg, pulling her jeans up. Some of Cam's leg got exposed. It was a pretty ropey sort of leg if you ask me. A bit hairy for a start. My mum always shaves her legs, and she wears sheer see-through tights to show them off. This Cam had socks like a schoolgirl. Only they were quite funny brightly

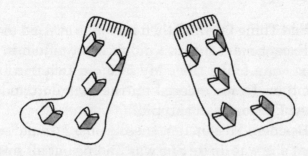

patterned socks. I thought the red and yellow
bits were just squares at first, but then I got a
bit closer and saw they were books. I wouldn't
mind having a pair of socks like that myself, if
I'm going to write all these books.

She's written books. Old Cammy. Cammy-
knicker, ha-ha. The other kids asked her and
she told them. She said she wrote some stories
but they didn't sell much so she also wrote some
romantic stuff. She doesn't look the romantic
type to me.

Adele got interested then because she loves
all those soppy love books and Cam told her
some titles and the boys all tittered and went
yuck yuck and Jenny got a bit narked but Cam
said she didn't mind, they were mostly yuck but
she couldn't help it if that's what people liked to
read.

Then they all started talking about reading.
Maxy said he liked this book *Where the Wild
Things Are* because the boy in that is called Max,
and Cam said she knew that book and she made

a Wild Thing face and then everyone else did too.

Except me. I mean, I didn't want to join in a dopey game like that. My face did twitch a bit but then I remembered all the make-up and I knew I'd look really stupid.

Besides, I'd got her sussed out. I could see what she was up to. She was finding out all sorts of things about all the kids without asking any nosy questions. Maxy went on about his dad being a Wile Thing. Adele went on about love, only of course real life wasn't like that, and love didn't ever last and people split up and sometimes didn't even go on loving their children.

Even little creepy Peter piped up about these Catherine Cookson books that his nan used to like, and he told Cam how he used to read them to her because her eyes had gone all blurry. And then *his* eyes went a bit blurry too, remembering his nan, and Cam's hand reached out sort of awkwardly. She didn't quite manage to hold his hand, she just sort of tapped his bony wrist sympathetically.

'My nan's dead too. And my mum. They're both together in heaven now. Angels, like,' said Louise, lisping a bit.

She always does that. Puts on this sweet little baby act when there are grown-ups about. Like she was a little angel herself. Ha. Our little Louise can be even worse than me when she wants. She's had three foster placements, no, was it four? Anyway, none of them worked out. But Louise always swore she didn't care. We used to have this pact that we'd do our best not to get fostered at all and we'd stay together at the Home till we got to be eighteen and then we'd get them to house us together. In our own modern flat. We'd got it all planned out. Louise even started thinking about our furniture, the ornaments, the posters on the walls.

And then Justine came and everything was spoilt. Oh how I hate that Justine Littlewood. I'm glad I broke her silly Mickey Mouse alarm clock. I'd like to break her into little bits and all.

Anyway, Louise lisped on about angels and I'll give that Cam her due, she didn't go all simpering and sentimental and pat Louise on her curly head and talk about the little darling. She stayed calm and matter-of-fact, and started talking about angels and wondering what they would look like.

'That's simple, Miss. They've got these big wings and long white nighties and those gold plate things stuck on the back of their heads,' said Justine.

'Draw one for me,' said Cam, offering her pen and notebook.

'OK,' said Justine, though she can't draw for

toffee. Then she had a close look at the pen in her hand. 'Here, it's a Mickey Mouse pen. Look, Louise, see the little Mickey. Oh Miss, where did you get this pen? It's great! I love Mickey, I do. I've got this Mickey Mouse alarm clock, my dad gave it me, only some *pig* broke it deliberately.' Justine looked over her shoulder and glared at me.

I glared back, making out I couldn't care less. And I *couldn't*. My face started burning, but that was just because of my mohair sweater.

Justine drew her stupid angel and Cam nodded at it.

'Yes, that's the way people usually draw angels.' She looked at Louise. 'So is this the way you imagine your mum and your nan?'

'Well. Sort of,' said Louise.

'Is that the sort of nightie that your nan would wear? And what about the halo, the gold plate bit. Would that fit neatly on top of her hairstyle?'

Louise giggled uncertainly, not sure what she was getting at.

'You draw me what you think your mum and nan look like as angels,' said Cam.

Louise started, but she can't draw much either, and she kept scribbling over what she'd done.

'This is silly,' she said, giving up.

I knew what Cam was on about. I'd have done a really great drawing of Louise's mum and nan in natty angel outfits. Like this.

'I'll draw you an angel, Miss,' said Maxy, grabbing at the pen. I'll draw me as an angel and I'll have big wings so I can fly like an aeroplane, y-e-e-e-o-o-o-w, y-e-e-e-o-o-o-w.' He went on making his dopey aeroplane noises all the time he was drawing.

Then the others had a go, even the big ones. I got a bit nearer and craned my neck to see what they'd all drawn. I didn't think any of them very inspired.

I knew exactly what I'd draw if she asked me. It wouldn't be a silly old angel.

Then Cam looked up. She caught my eye. She did ask me.

'Have a go?' she said, dead casual.

I gave this little shrug as if I couldn't care less. Then I sauntered forward, very slowly. I held out my hand for the pen.

'This is Tracy,' said Jenny, poking her big nose in. 'She's the one who wants to be a writer.'

I felt my face start burning again.

'What, her?' said Justine. 'You've got to be joking.'

'Now Justine,' said Jenny. 'Tracy's written heaps and heaps in her Life Book.'

'Yeah, but it's all rubbish,' said Justine, and

her hand shot out and she made a grab underneath my jumper, where I was keeping this book for safety. I bashed out at her but I wasn't quick enough. She snatched the book from me before I could stop her.

'Give that here!' I shrieked.

'It's rubbish, I tell you, listen,' said Justine, and she opened my book and started reading in a silly high-pitched baby voice "Once upon a time there was a little girl called Tracy Beaker and that sounds stupid and no wonder because *I am* stupid and I wet the bed and— Ooooowwww!'"

Things got a bit hazy after that. But I got my book back. And Justine's nose became a wonderful scarlet fountain. I was glad glad glad. I wanted her whole body to spout blood but Jenny had hold of me by this time and she was shouting for Mike and I got hauled off to the Quiet Room. Only I wasn't quiet in there. I yelled my head off. I went on yelling when Jenny came to try and calm me down. And then Jenny went away and someone else came into the room. I wasn't sure who it was at first because when I yell my eyes screw up and I can't see properly. Then I made out the jeans and the T-shirt and the shock of hair and I knew it was Cam Whotsit and that made me burn all over until I felt like a junior Joan of Arc.

There was me, throwing a hairy fit, and there was her standing there watching me. I don't care about people like Jenny or Elaine seeing me. They're used to it. Nearly all children in care have a roaring session once in a while. I have them more than once, actually. And I usually just let rip, but now I felt like a right raving loony in front of her.

But I didn't stop yelling all the same. There was no point. She'd already seen me at it. And heard me too. She didn't try to stop me. She wasn't saying a word. She was standing there. And she had this awful expression on her face. I couldn't stand it. She looked sorry for me.

I wasn't having that. So I told her to go away. That's putting it politely. I yelled some very rude words at her. And she just sort of shrugged and nodded and went off.

I was left screaming and swearing away, all by myself.

But I'm OK now. I'm not in the Quiet Room any more. I stayed in there ever such a long time and I even had my tea in there on a tray but now I'm in my bedroom and I've been writing and writing and writing away and it looks like I can't *help* being a writer. I've written so much I've got a big lump on the longest finger of my right hand. You look.

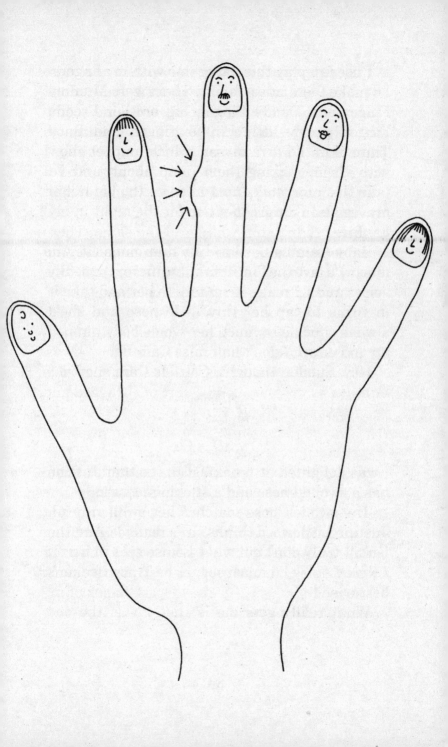

I used to play this daft game with my fingers. I'd make them into a family. There were Mummy Finger and Daddy Finger, big brother Freddy Finger, pretty little Pinkie Finger, and Baby Thumbkin. I'd give myself a little puppet show with them, making them jump about, and I'd take them for walks up and down the big hill of my leg and I'd tuck them up for the night in my hankie.

Baby Camilla used to like that game ever so much. I'd give the Finger family different squeaky voices and I'd make them talk to her and take it in turns to tap her tiny little nose and she'd always chuckle so much her whole body jumped up and down. I don't half miss Camilla.

Hey. Sudden thought. Cam. Is Cam short for *Camilla*?

I was delighted at breakfast to see that Justine has a swollen nose and a sticking plaster.

The swollen nose matches her swollen head. Justine Littlewood thinks she's really it. And she isn't. I truly don't get what Louise sees in her. If *I* were Louise I'd much sooner be Tracy Beaker's best friend.

What really gets me is that I was the one

who palled up with Justine first. She turned up at the Home one evening, all down and droopy because her mum had cleared off with some bloke and left Justine and her two little brothers and her dad to get on with it. Only her dad couldn't get on with it, and the kids got taken into care. The brothers got into a short-term foster home because they were still nearly at the baby stage and not too much bother. But Justine didn't get taken on too, because they thought she'd be difficult.

I generally like kids who are difficult. And I thought I liked the look of Justine. And the sound of her. Because after the first droopy evening she suddenly found her tongue and she started sounding off at everyone, getting really stroppy and swearing. She knew even more swear words than I do.

She was like that all week but she shut up on Sunday. Her dad was supposed to see her on Sunday. She was sitting waiting for him right after breakfast, though he wasn't supposed to be coming till eleven o'clock. Eleven came and went. And twelve. And then it was dinnertime and Justine wouldn't eat her chicken. She sat at the window all afternoon, not budging.

My tummy went tight whenever I looked at her. I knew what it was like. I used to sit like that. Not just here. I used to wait at both my crummy foster homes. And the children's homes in between. Waiting for my mum to come.

But now I've got myself sorted out. No more dumb sitting about for me. Because my mum's probably too far away to come on a quick visit. Yeah, that's it, she's probably abroad somewhere, she's always fancied travelling.

She's maybe in France.

Or Spain, she likes sunshine.

What am I thinking of? She'll have gone to

the States. Maybe Hollywood. My mum looks so great she'd easily get into the movies.

You can't hop on a bus and visit your daughter

when you're hundreds and thousands of miles away in Hollywood, now can you?

All the same, even though I don't sit waiting,

I always go a bit tingly when there's a knock at the door. I hold my breath, waiting to see who it is, just in case …

So I could understand what old Justine was going through. I didn't try to talk to her because I knew she'd snap my head off, but I sort of sidled up to her and dropped a lollipop on her lap and backed away. It wasn't exactly my lollipop. I'd snaffled several from little Wayne. His dopey mum is younger than Adele and she hasn't got a clue about babies. Whenever she comes she brings Wayne lollipops. Well, they've got sticks, haven't they? We don't want little Wayne giving himself a poke in the eye. And he's normally so drooly that if you add a lot of lolly-lick as well he gets stickier than Superglue. So it's really a kindness to nick his lollies when he's not looking.

'But why did you want to give one to that Justine?' Louise asked. 'She's horrible, Tracy. She barged right into me on the stairs yesterday and she didn't even say sorry, she just called me a very rude word indeed.' Louise whispered it primly.

'Um. Did she really say that?' I said, giggling. 'Oh she's not so bad really. And anyway, I didn't give her the *red* lollipop. I saved that for you.'

'Thanks, Trace,' said Louise, and she beamed at me.

Oh we were like *that* in those days.

I kept an eye on Justine. She didn't budge for a good half hour, letting the lollipop lie in her lap. And then I saw her hand creep out. She unwrapped it and gave it one small suspicious lick, as if I'd poisoned it. But it must have tasted OK because she took another lick, and then another, and then she settled down for a good long suck. Lollipops can be very soothing to the stomach.

She didn't say thank you or anything. And when she eventually had to give up waiting and go to bed she stalked off by herself. But the next day at breakfast she gave me this little nod. So I nodded back and flicked one cornflake in her direction and she flicked one back, and we ended up having this good game of tiddlyflakes and after that we were friends. Not best friends.

Louise was my best friend. Ha.

She moaned at first.

'Why do we have to have that Justine hanging round us all the time?' she complained. 'I don't like her, Trace. She's dead tough.'

'Well, I want to be tough too. You've got to be tough. What do you mean, *I'm* tougher than Justine,' I said, sticking my chin out.

'Nutter,' said Louise.

It started to get to me though. I started swearing worse than Justine and Jenny got really mad at me because Maxy started copying me and even little Wayne would come out with a right mouthful when he felt like it.

So then I started the Dare Game. I've always won any dare. Until Justine came along.

I dared her to say the rudest word she could think of when the vicar came on a visit. And she did.

She dared me to go out in the garden stark naked. And I did.

I dared her to eat a worm. And she did.
She dared *me* to eat a worm.

I said that wasn't fair. She couldn't copy my

dare. Louise opened her big mouth and said that I hated worms. 'Then I dare her to eat *two* worms,' said Justine. So I did.

I *did*. Sort of. It wasn't my fault they made me sick. I did swallow them first. Justine said I just

spat them out straight away but I *didn't*.

I thought hard. I happen to be a crack hand at skateboarding. Justine's not much good at getting her balance and her steering's rotten. So I fixed up this skateboard assault course round the garden, with sloping benches and all sorts. And I dared Justine to have a go. So she did.

She fell over a lot. But she kept getting up and carrying on. So I said she was disqualified.

But Louise said Justine should still win the bet
if she completed the course. And she did.

Then Justine dared me to climb the tree at
the end of the garden. So I did. It wasn't *my*

fault I didn't get right to the top. I didn't ask that stupid Mike to interfere. But Justine said I'd lost that dare, and Louise backed her up. I couldn't believe my ears. Louise was *my* friend. We couldn't do any more dares because Jenny PUT HER FOOT DOWN. You don't argue when she does that.

The next day Justine's famous dad put in an appearance at long last. Justine had gone on

and on about how good-looking he was, just like a pop star, and he actually had an evening job singing in pubs, which was why he couldn't be at home to look after her and her brothers. Well, you should have seen him. Starting to go bald. Pot belly. Medallion. He wasn't *quite* wearing a frilly shirt and flares, but almost.

You wouldn't catch me wanting a dad like that. But Justine gave a weird little whoop when she saw him and jumped up into his arms like a great big baby. He took her on some dumb outing and when she got back she was all bubbly and bouncy and showing off this . . . this present he'd bought her.

I don't know why, but I felt really narked at
Justine. It was all right when she didn't get a

← whoops!

visit, like us lot. But now I kept picking on her
and saying silly sniggery things about her dad.
And then she burst into tears.

I was a bit shocked. I didn't say anything *that*
bad. And I never thought a really tough girl like
Justine would ever cry. *I* don't ever cry, no matter
what. I mean, my mum hasn't managed to come
and visit me for donkey's years and I don't even
have a dad, but catch me crying.

And then I got another shock. Because
Louise turned on me.

'You are horrid, Tracy,' she said. And then
she put her arms right round Justine and gave
her a big hug. 'Don't take any notice of her.
She's just jealous.'

Me, jealous? Of Justine? Of Justine's dopey
dumb dad? She had to be joking.

But it didn't look like she was joking. She
and Justine went off together, their arms round
each other.

I told myself I didn't care. Although I did care a little bit then. And I did wonder if I'd gone over the top with my remarks. I can have a very cutting tongue.

I thought I'd smooth things over at breakfast.

Maybe even tell Justine I hadn't really meant any of it. Not actually apologize, of course, but show her that I was sorry. But it was too late. I was left on my own at breakfast. Louise didn't sit next to me in her usual seat. She went and sat at the table by the window – with Justine.

'Hey, Louise,' I called. And then I called again, louder. 'Have you gone deaf or something?' I yelled.

But she could hear me all right. She just wasn't talking to me. She wasn't my best friend any more. She was Justine's.

All I've got is silly squitty twitty Peter Ingham. Oh, maybe he's not so bad. I was writing all this down when there was this tiny tapping at my door. As if some timid little insect was scrabbling away out there. I told this beetle to buzz off because I was busy, but it went on scribble-scrabbling. So eventually I heaved myself off my bed and went to see what it wanted.

'Do you want to play, Tracy?' he said.

'Play?' I said witheringly. 'What do you think I am, Peter Ingham? Some kind of infant? I'm busy writing.' But I'd been writing so much my whole arm ached and my writing lump was all red and throbbing. Oh, how we writers suffer for our art! It's chronic, it really is.

So I did just wonder if it was time for a little diversion.

'What sort of games do *you* play then, little Peetle-Beetle?'

He blinked a bit and shuffled backwards as if I was about to squash him, but he managed to squeak out something about paper games.

'Paper games?' I said. 'Oh, I see. Do we make a football out of paper and then give it a kick so that it blows away? What fun. Or do we make a dear little teddy out of paper and give it a big hug and squash it flat? Even better.'

Peter giggled nervously. 'No, Tracy, pen and paper games. I always used to play noughts and crosses with my nan.'

'Oh gosh, how incredibly thrilling,' I said.

Beetles don't understand sarcasm.

'Good, *I* like noughts and crosses too,' he said, producing a pencil out of his pocket.

There was no deterring him. So we played paper games after that.

I suppose it passed the time a bit. And now I've just spotted something. Right at the bottom of the page, in teeny tiny beetle writing, there's a little message.

Guess what! I've got a letter!

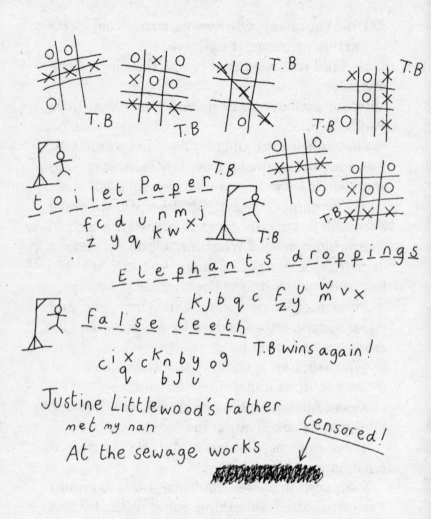

T.B

T.B

T.B

T.B

T.B

toilet Paper   T.B

f c d u n m j
z y q k w x

T.B

Elephants droppings

k j b q c f u w v x
z y m

false teeth

c i x c k n b y o g   T.B wins again!
q   b J u

Justine Littlewood's father
met my nan

At the sewage works   Censored!
                              ↓

I don't half like
you, Tracy.
signed Peter Ingham.

100

Not another soppy little message from Peter. A real private letter that came in the post, addressed to Ms Tracy Beaker.

I haven't had many letters just recently. Oh, there have been plenty of letters *about* me. Elaine's got a whole library of files on me. I've had a secret rifle through them and you should just see some of the mean horrid things they say about me. I had a good mind to sue them for libel. Yeah, that would be great. And I'd get awarded all these damages, hundreds of thousands of pounds, and I'd be able to thumb my nose at Justine and Jenny and Elaine and all the others. I'd just clutch my lovely lolly in my hot little hand and go off and ...

Well, I'd have my own house, right? And I'd employ someone to foster me. But because I'd be paying them, *they'd* have to do everything *I* said. I'd order them to make me a whole birthday cake to myself every single day of the week and they'd just have to jump to it and do so.

I wouldn't let anybody else in to share it with me.

Not even Peter. I had to share my *real* birthday cake with him. And he gave me a nudge and said 'What's the matter, Tracy? Don't you feel well?' just when I'd closed my eyes tight and was in the middle of making my birthday wish. So it

got all muddled and I lost my thread and now if my mum doesn't come for me it's all that Peter Ingham's fault.

Well, maybe it is.

But I'd still let him come round to my house sometimes and we could play paper games. They're quite good fun really, because I always win.

Who else could I have in my house? I could try and get Camilla. I'd look after her. I could get a special playpen and lots of toys. I've always liked the look of all that baby junk. I don't suppose I had much of that sort of thing when I was a baby. Yeah, I could have a proper nursery in my house and when Camilla

wasn't using it I could muck about in there, just
for a laugh.

I wonder if Camilla remembers me now?
That's the trouble with babies.

I wonder if Cam *is* short for Camilla?
That's who my letter was from.

I was a bit disappointed at first. I thought it

was from my mum. I know she's never written to me before but still, when Jenny handed it to me at breakfast I just clutched at the envelope and held it tight and shut my eyes quick because they got suddenly hot and prickly and if I was a snivelly sort of person I might well have cried.

'What's up with Tracy?' the other kids mumbled.

I gave a great swallow and sniff and opened my eyes and said, 'Nothing's up! Look, I've got a letter! A letter from—'

'I think it's maybe from Cam Lawson,' Jenny said, very quickly indeed.

I caught my breath. 'Yeah. Cam Lawson. See that? She's written me my own personal letter. And she's not written to any of you lot. See! She's written to *me*.'

'So what does she say then?'

'Never you mind. It's *private*.'

I went off to read it all by myself. I didn't get around to it for a bit. I was thinking all these dopey things about my mum. And I had a bad attack of hay fever. And I didn't really want to read what Cam Lawson had to say anyway. She saw me having my hairy fit. I was scared she'd think me some sort of loony.

Only the letter was OK.

10 Beech Road
Kingtown

Dear Tracy

   We didn't really get together properly when I
came on my visit. It was a pity because Jenny told
me a bit about you and I liked the sound of you.
She said you're very naughty and you like writing.

   I'm exactly the opposite. I've
always been very very good. Especially
when I was at school. You wouldn't half
have teased me.

   I'm not quite so good now, thank goodness.

   And I hate writing. Because it's what I do for
a living and every day I get up from my cornflakes
and go and sit at my typewriter and my hands clench
into fists and I go cross-eyed staring at the blank
paper – and I think – what a stupid way to earn a
living. Why don't I do something else? Only I'm
useless at everything else so I just have to carry
on with my writing.

   Are you carrying on with your writing? You're
telling your own story? An actual autobiography?
Most girls your age wouldn't have much to write
about, but you're lucky in that respect because so
many different things have happened to you.

   Good luck with it.

      Yours,

      Cam

Lee Road Dumping
Ground for Difficult Kids

Dear Ms Lawson,
        Jenny says that's what I should
call you, Ms Lawson, although you wrote Cam
at the bottom of your letter. What sort of name is
Cam? If you're called Camilla then I think that's
a lovely name and don't see why you want to muck
it up. I had a friend in this other home called
Camilla and she liked her name. I had a special way
of saying it, Ca-miiii-lla, and she'd always
giggle. She was only a baby but very bright.
                Why don't you mind me being naughty?
Actually, its not always my fault that I get
into trouble. People just pick on me. Lots of
people, but I won't name names because I don't
tell tales, not like some people.

Do you like my drawing? I
liked yours, I thought they
were funny. What do you
mean, you hate writing?

Tracy Beaker did this.
Tracy Beaker did that.
Um Tracy Beaker is
awful!

GLUE

I think that's weird when it's what you do. I like writing. I think it's ever so easy. I just start and it goes on and on. The only trouble is that it hurts your hand and you get a big lump on your finger. And ink all over your hand and clothes and paper if some clueless toddler has been chewing on your felt tip. Are you having trouble writing your article about us? I could help you if you liked. I can tell you anything you need to know about me. And the others. How about it?

Yes I am still writing my autobiography. I like that word. I asked Jenny and she said it's a story about yourself, and that's right, that's exactly what I'm writing. I'd let you have a look at it but it's strictly personal. Don't take any notice of what that moron Justine read out. There are some really good bits, honest.

Yours
From your fellow writer

Tracy Beaker

R.S.V.P
That means you've got to reply.

10 Beech Road.

Dear Tracy,

Thanks for your lovely letter. It made me laugh. Do you know what? I think you're a born writer.

I could do with some help on my feature.

Are you around next Saturday morning? Hope to see you then. Cam.

I hate Camilla. I used to get teased rotten at school for having such a soppy name.

The dumping Ground.

Dear Camilla,

It's not a soppy name. You've got to be proud of it. You want to try having a name like Tracy Beaker. Excuse this crummy writing paper. Jenny lent me the first lot but she says I'm costing her a small fortune in paper and can't I give it a rest. So I borrowed this from one of the little ones. Isn't it yucky? I know.

This is Goblinda the Goblin and she's going to gob all over these daft fairies.

Yes, I'll help you out on Saturday. If I'm there, of course.

My Mum often comes to take me out. Although she may be abroad just now. I think she's going to take me on a trip abroad too. But it mightn't be for a while, so I'll see you on Saturday morning probably. About what time? We have breakfast at 8.30 on Saturdays and I always eat quickly so about 8.35?

Yours, from your fellow - hang on, I'm not a fellow

Yours, from another lady writer,

Tracy

R.S.V.P
So as I know what time to start waiting.

10 Beech Road

Dear Sister Writer,

See you Saturday morning. 8·35 impossible.
I look like this at 8·35.

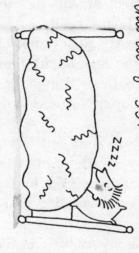

How about 10·35?
Cam. Sorry. Camilla. Ugh!

P.S. I love Goblinda. Put her in a story.

Imagine staying in your bed half the morning. She is lazy. And she was late even then. It was 10.41 before she turned up. I'd practically given her up. She's supposed to be a professional writer and yet she can't even keep an appointment on time.

She's pretty hopeless if you ask me. She didn't half muck up this morning. I'd got it all worked out. I was ready to fill her in on all the facts. Mostly about me, of course. But I thought maybe she might fancy interviewing Peter too, to balance things up. A girl's point of view, and a boy's. No need to bother with any of the others.

Cam's got this dinky little tape recorder and after just one minute of instruction I mastered all the mechanism and had great fun fast-forwarding and rewinding and playing back. I had a little go first, trying out all my different accents, doing my Australian G'day routine and my American gangster and my special Donald Duck, but then I decided we'd better get down to business and as I'm not the sort of girl to hog the limelight I said Peter could go first.

He backed away from the tape recorder as if it was a loaded gun.

'Don't be so silly, Peter. Just act normal and speak into it.'

'What shall I say?' Peter squeaked.

I sighed impatiently. 'Just tell Cam your life story.'

'But I haven't got a story. I couldn't think of anything to put when Elaine gave me that book,' said Peter. 'I lived with my nan. And she died. So I came here. That's all there is.'

'That's OK, Peter. Don't let Tracy bully you into it. You don't have to say anything,' said Cam.

'What a cheek! I'm not a bully. Huh, *I* was the kid who always *got* bullied. This other Home I was in, there was this huge great teenage bloke, and he was a really tough skinhead and he had these bovver boots and I filled them up with custard for a joke and he didn't see the funny

113

side of it and yet he didn't half look hilarious, all this frothy yellow liquid squishing up his trouser legs – so anyway, from then on my name was mud, and he really had it in for me. The things he used to do!'

I was about to launch into a long account but typical typical that Justine Littlewood came barging over.

'It's not fair, Miss. You're letting that stupid Tracy show off like mad, and you're not giving any of us a go.'

'You shut your face, blabbermouth,' I said. 'She's not come to see you lot. She's come to see *me*. A strictly private appointment. So clear off. Isn't that right, Cam?'

'Well. Yes, I've come to talk to you, Tracy. But we could all have a go on the tape recorder for a bit,' she said.

What a gutless creep she is. She was there just to see *me*. We had a proper business appointment. All she had to do was tell Justine and the others to buzz off. It wouldn't have mattered if Peter stayed, because he's not really any bother. But the others! It was useless. Practically the whole morning was wasted. She let them all muck around on the tape recorder and then some of the littlies wanted another go drawing with her Mickey Mouse pen, and then

Jenny came in with coffee for Cam and coke for us and it was like some big party. Only I didn't feel like the birthday girl. I felt squeezed out to the edge again.

After a bit I stomped off. I kept looking back over my shoulder and I thought she didn't even notice. But then she sidled up. She still had baby Becky on one hip and little Wayne clinging to her leg like a limpet. She gave me a dig in the back with her Mickey Mouse pen.

'Hey,' she said softly. 'Shall we get started on your interview now, Tracy?'

'Well, you've got all these other kids. Why waste your time with me?' I said acidly. 'I mean, I'm only the one you were *supposed* to see.'

'Tell you what. Let's go up to your room. Just you and me. How about it?'

'OK,' I said, yawning and shrugging. 'If you really want. I've gone off the idea now. But if you insist. Just for a minute or two.'

It took her a while to dump the baby and prise Wayne away, and then all the others kept clustering around, saying it wasn't fair. So do you know what she did? She said they could do interviews on her tape recorder. And she put *Justine* in charge of it.

'You aren't half making a mistake there, Cam. You're crazy. They'll wreck it in two minutes,' I said.

'No they won't. Justine will work it. And everyone take a two-minute turn. Introduce yourselves first, and then say whatever you want. But don't worry, Peter, you don't have to.'

'You are stark staring mad,' I said. 'Look, if anyone's in charge of that tape recorder it's got to be me. I'm the only one who knows how to work it properly.

'Well, show Justine,' said Cam. 'Then she'll be able to work it too.'

'I'm not showing *her*,' I said. But in the end I

did. And of course Justine was clueless and didn't catch on and I kept sighing and groaning and she got narked and gave me a push and I clenched my fist ready to give her a thump but Cam got in between us and said, 'Look, I'll run through it. Here's the record button, Justine, right?' and *eventually* Justine got the hang of it. I don't know why she's called Littlewood. Little*brain* would be far more appropriate.

Then Cam and I went up to my room and left them to it.

'You thought you'd found a way of getting Justine and me to make friends,' I said. 'But, ha-ha, it didn't work, did it? Because we're always going to be deadly enemies.'

Cam laughed at me. She laughed at the notice taped on my bedroom door too.

THIS ROOM BELONGS TO
TRACY BEAKER
STRICTLY PRIVATE
KEEP OUT ON PAIN OF DEATH.
AND IT WILL BE A VERY PAINFUL
DEATH TOO.

'It's OK. You can come in. You're my guest,' I said, opening the door for her.

My room looked a bit of a tip actually. I hadn't got round to making the bed and the floor was littered with socks and pyjama tops and bits of biscuit and pencil sharpenings, so she had to pick her way through. She didn't make a big thing of it though. She looked at all the stuff I've got pinned to my noticeboard, and she nodded a bit and smiled.

'Is that your mum?' Cam asked.

'Isn't she lovely? You'd really think she was a film star, wouldn't you? I think she maybe *is* a film star now. In Hollywood. And she'll be jetting over to see me soon. Maybe she'll take me back with her, and I'll get to be a film star too. A child star. The marvellous movie moppet, Tracy Beaker. Yeah. That would be great, eh?'

I spun around with a great grin, doing a cutsie-pie curtsey – and Cam caught on straight away and started clapping and acting like an adoring fan.

'I hope you're still going to be a writer too,' she said. 'Have you done any more about Goblinda?'

'Give us a chance. I've been too busy doing my autobiography,' I said.

'I suppose this autobiography of yours is strictly private?' Cam asked, sounding a bit wistful.

'Of course it is,' I said. But then I hesitated. Elaine the Pain has seen bits of it. And Louise and Littlebrain. And I did show a bit to Peter actually, just to show him how much I'd done. So why shouldn't I show a bit to Cam too? As she's a sort of friend.

So I let her have a few peeps. I had to be a bit careful, because some of the stuff I've written about her isn't exactly flattering. She came across a description of her by accident, but she didn't take offence. She roared with laughter.

'You really should be the one writing this article about children in care, Tracy, not me. I think you'd make a far better job of it.'

'Yes, have you made a start on this article yet?'

She fidgeted a bit. 'Not really. It's difficult. You see, this magazine editor wants a very touching sentimental story about all these sad sweet vulnerable little children that will make her readers reach for a wad of Kleenex.'

'Yeah, that's the right approach.'

'Oh come off it, Tracy. None of you lot are at all *sweet*. You're all gutsy and stroppy and spirited. I want to write what you're really like but it won't be the sort of thing the editor wants.'

'And it won't be the sort of thing *I* want either. You've got to make me sound sweet, Cam! No-one will want me otherwise. I've gone past my sell-by date already. It gets hopeless when you get older than five or six. You've stopped being a cute little toddler and started to be difficult. And I'm not pretty either so people won't take one look at my photo and start cooing. And then it's not like I'm up for adoption so people can't ever make me their little girl, not properly.'

'You're not up for adoption because you've still got your mum?'

'Exactly. And like I said, she'll be coming for me soon, but meanwhile I'd like to live in a proper homey home instead of this old dump. Otherwise I'll get institutionalized.'

Cam's eyebrows go up.

'I know what it means and all. I've heard Elaine and some of the other social workers going on about it. It's when you get so used to living in an institution like this that you never learn how to live in a proper home. And when you get to eighteen you can't cope and you don't know how to do your own shopping or cooking or anything. Although I can't see me ever having that problem. I bet I could cope right this minute living on my own. They'd just have to bung me the lolly and I'd whizz off down the shops and have a whale of a time.'

'I bet you would,' said Cam.

Then Maxy started scratching at my door and

whining and complaining. I told him to push off, because Cam and I were In Conference, but he didn't take any notice.

'Miss, Miss, it's not fair, them big girls won't let me have a go on the tape, I want a go, Miss, you tell them to let me have a go, they're playing they're pop stars, Miss, and *I* want a go.'

Cam smiled and sighed, looking at her watch.

'I'd better go back downstairs. I've got to be going in a minute anyway.'

'Oh that's not fair! Aren't you staying? You can have lunch with us lot, Jenny won't mind, and it's hamburgers on Saturday.'

'No, I'm meeting someone for lunch in the town.'

'Oh. Where are you going then?'

'Well, we'll probably have a drink and then we'll have a salad or something. My friend fusses about her figure.'

'Who wants boring old salad? If I was having lunch out I'd go to McDonald's. I'd have a Big Mac and French fries and a strawberry milkshake. See, I'm not the slightest bit institutionalized, am I?'

'You've been to McDonald's then?'

'Oh, heaps of times,' I said. And then I paused. 'Well, not actually *inside*. I was fostered with this boring family, Julie and Ted, and I kept on at them to take me, but they said it was junk food. And I said all their boring brown beans and soggy veggy stews were the *real* junk because they looked like someone had already eaten them and sicked them up and – well, anyway, they never took me.'

'No wonder,' said Cam, grinning.

'I am allowed to go out to lunch from here, you know.'

'Are you?'

'Yes. Any day. And tell you what, I really will work on that article for you. I could work on it this week and show you what I've done. And we could discuss it. Over lunch. At McDonald's. Hint, hint, hint.'

Cam smacked the side of her head as if a great thought has just occurred to her.

'Hey, Tracy! Would you like to come out with me to McDonald's next week?'

'Yes please!' I pause. 'Really?' You're not kidding?'

'Really. Next Saturday. I'll come and pick you up about twelve, OK?'

'I'll be waiting.'

And so I shall. I'd better send her a letter too, just in case she forgets.

The dumping ground.

Dear Camilla,
I'm working hard on the article.
I'll show you on Saturday. Remember we have
a lunch-date. At 12. To go to McDonald's.
From your co-writer Tracy Beaker.

P.S Goblinda says if you took her to
McDonald's she'd be ever so good and wouldn't
gob once.

I know she said twelve o'clock. And she's not exactly the most punctual of people. She mightn't get here till ten past. Even twenty or half past. So why am I sitting here staring out of the window when we've only just had breakfast?

I hate waiting. It really gets on my nerves. I can't concentrate on anything. Not even my writing. And I haven't done any writing in this book all week because I've been so busy with my article for Cam. I've got it all finished now and even though I say it myself I've done a really great job. She can just bung it at her editor and no-one will be any the wiser. I should really get the whole fee for it myself. But I'm very generous. I'll share fifty fifty with Cam, because she's my friend.

Old Pete's my friend too. We've been bumping into each other in the middle of the night this week, on a sheet sortie. Mostly we just had a little whisper but last night I found him all huddled up and soggy because he'd had a nightmare about his nan. Strangely enough, I'd had a nightmare about my mum and it had brought on a bad attack of my hay fever. Normally I like to keep to myself at such moments as some stupid ignorant twits think my red eyes and runny nose are because I've been crying. And I never *ever* cry, no matter what.

But I knew Peter wouldn't tease me so I huddled down beside him for a bit and when I felt him shivering I put my arm round him and told him he was quite possibly my best friend ever.

He's just come up to me now and asked if I want to play paper games. Yeah, it might pass the time.

Oh charming! Peter and I had just got started

_ A _ _ I L L A _ L A _ _ _ O N

B K U D E Y J P S T R Y

and I was about to win the first game when Elaine the Pain comes buzzing in. She's here dumping off some boring new kid and now she wants to have a little chat with Peter.

'Well, tough, Elaine, because *I'm* having a little chat with Peter right now,' I said.

'Now now Tracy,' said Elaine.

'Yes, *now*,' I said.

Elaine bared her teeth at me. That smile means she'd really like to give me a clip around the ear but she's going to make allowances for me.

'I expect you're feeling a bit het up this morning, Tracy, because of this writer coming to take you out. Jenny's told me all about it. It'll be a lovely treat for you.'

'You bet. And it'll be a lovely treat for her too because I've written this article for her.'

'Well, I might have a little treat up my sleeve for Peter here,' Elaine said, and she shuffled him off into a corner and started talking to him earnestly.

She's still talking to him. She's keeping her voice down. But I can have very large waggly ears when I want. Elaine's going on about these people she knows. An older couple whose children have all grown up. And now they're a bit lonely. They'd like to look after someone.

A little boy. Maybe a little boy just like Peter.

So that's it. Little Peetie-Weetie is obviously going to get fostered and live Happily Ever After.

Well, that's good, isn't it? Because he's my best friend.

No, it's bad, because he won't be able to be my best friend any more if he goes off and gets himself fostered.

And it's not fair. He's hardly been here any time. I've been here ages and ages and no-one ever wants to foster me now.

Still, who wants to be fostered by some boring older couple anyway? Older might mean really ancient. And crabby. And strict. They'd never wear jeans or write funny letters or take Peter to McDonald's.

I wish Cam would hurry up and come for me. Although it's nowhere near time. It's daft me sitting here by the window like this. Waiting.

Justine is hovering behind me. I think she's waiting for her dad. I hope she won't tell him about the little accident to her Mickey Mouse clock. He might come and beat me up. Even though the clock's all mended now. Jenny took it in to this shop and they sorted it. I was glad to see old Mickey tick-tocking round and round again. Justine caught me looking and she gave me this great fierce push that nearly knocked me over and told me that if I so much as touched her clock again she'd duff me up good and proper. Honestly! My fists clenched and I was all set to have a real go at her because no-one talks to Tracy Beaker like that, but then I remembered my lunch date. Jenny isn't best pleased with me at the moment. If I got into a punch-up with Justine then she mightn't let me go out with Cam.

So I Kept Calm. I smiled at Justine in a superior sort of way.

'Really Justine, do you always have to resort to violence?' I said.

My superior willpower was wasted on Justine. She just thought I was chicken.

'Cowardy cowardy custard,' she's mumbling under her breath now. 'Tracy Beaker's got no bottle.'

I shan't take any notice of her. I shall just sit here writing. And waiting. It's not *that* long now. Only it seems like for ever.

I used to sit like this. When I waited for my mum. I wonder when she will come. I had that awful dream about her. I was out having lunch with Cam in McDonald's and it was really great and we were having a smashing time together when I looked up at the clock and saw it had gone one o'clock, and it suddenly rang a terrible bell in my head, and I remembered that my

mum was coming to take me to lunch at one o'clock, and I just went panic panic panic.

I charged off to try to get back to the Home in time and I got a bus but they chucked me off because I didn't have enough money and then I ran into Aunty Peggy and she chased after me to give me a good smacking and Julie and Ted tripped me up and Justine caught me and threw me in a river and I couldn't swim and I was drowning . . . and then I woke up. Wet.

So OK, I know it was only a dopey old nightmare. But what if it was some kind of *premonition*??? What if my mum really comes for me today and I miss her because I'm having lunch with Cam?

I'll have to talk to Elaine.

Well, I've talked. Sort of.

'Can I have a little chat, Elaine?' I said.

'Tracy. I'm still having a little chat with Peter.'

'You've *had* a little chat with Peter. Correction. You've had an extremely long and boring endless conversation with him. And you're my social worker just as much as his. So could you *please* come and have a little chat with me. It's sort of urgent.'

Elaine sighed. She ruffled Peter's hair and gave him a little chuck under the chin. Then she came over to me at long last.

'What is it then, Tracy?'

I swallowed, not sure how to put it.

'Tracy, are you just winding me up?' said Elaine.

'No! It's just . . . Look, about my mum. She doesn't know I'm here, does she?'

'Well. No, I don't think so.'

'But if she wanted to find me she could, couldn't she?'

I said it in a whisper but Justine heard.

131

'Who'd ever want to come looking for you, Tracy Beaker?' she said.

'You shut your mouth!'

Justine pulled a hideous face and Louise giggled. Then she tugged at Justine's sleeve.

'Come on. Let's see what that new girl's doing. She's got two whole suitcases with her, so she must have heaps of clothes.'

But Justine wanted to stay at the window so Louise wandered off by herself. I knew Justine was still listening for all she was worth (honestly, some people have no decency whatsoever) but I had to keep on asking Elaine.

'If my mum wanted she could go round to that old children's home. And they could tell her where I am now, couldn't they?'

'Yes, of course they would,' said Elaine. 'Don't worry, Tracy. Each time you get moved on somewhere else, there's a special record kept. So if your mum wants to see you then it's easy. They look up your name and file number and find your present address.'

'Good,' I said.

'What's up, Tracy? You still look a bit worried.'

'I'm OK.'

Only I don't feel OK. What if my mum does come today? And I'm out having lunch with someone else? Will she wait for me? Or will she get fidgety and fed up and zoom off again? And I'll get back here and Jenny will say, 'Oh, by the way, Tracy, your mum called when you were out, but she couldn't wait for you. She was all set to take you back to Hollywood with her but she had this plane to catch so she couldn't hang about.'

What am I going to do?

Maybe she won't come today. She hasn't ever come before. And yet, what if she did? I *wish* I hadn't had that dream. Dreams *can* come true.

I feel sick. Maybe I don't really want to go to McDonald's after all.

See that? It's real blood.

I'm not going to get to go to McDonald's now, whether I want to or not. I've had a fight. I'm in the Quiet Room.

This is how it happened. I went over to Peter. I whispered in his ear.

'Would you like to go to McDonald's with Cam?'

Peter scrunched up his neck because my whispers can be a bit tickly.

'You mean, go with you?'

'No. Go instead of me. I've kind of gone off the idea. It's OK, I'll tell Cam when she comes. She quite likes you, so she won't mind taking you instead.'

Peter looked worried.

'I can't, Tracy. I'm going out too. With these people.'

'What, with this boring older couple?' I said.

Elaine raised her eyebrows at me but I took no notice.

'I bet they won't take you to McDonald's,' I said.

'Why don't *you* want to go, Tracy?' Elaine asked. 'I thought you were so looking forward to it.'

'Yes, but . . . I want to stay here. Just in case.'

Elaine is a pain but she's also quite quick at putting two and two together.

'Tracy, I don't think your mum will be coming today,' she said quietly.

'Oh. I know that. Only I had this dream. She did in the dream.'

'Yes, I'm sure she did. And I expect it was a lovely dream but—'

'No, it was a perfectly foul dream because I wasn't here to see her and—'

'And you woke up blubbing with a soaking wet bed, *baby*,' Justine muttered.

'I told you to shut *up*,' I said, getting really riled.

'I'd go out with your writer friend, Tracy,' said Elaine.

'Mm. Well. I'm not sure I really want to now, anyway.' I glare at Peter. 'Why do you have to be seeing this boring old couple today, eh? You could see them any old time. You go and have a Big Mac with Cam.'

Peter wriggled. Elaine put her hand on his shoulder. Her looked up at her and then at me.

'Sorry, Tracy. I want to meet them. Aunty Vi and Uncle Stanley.'

'Of course you want to meet them, Peter. And Tracy is going to meet her writer,' said Elaine.

'No, I'm not.'

'*I'd* go,' said Justine. 'Only I can't, because of my dad. I'm going out to lunch with him.'

'You were supposed to be going out with him last Saturday. Only he never turned up,' I said.

'OK, but he does come *sometimes*. Not like your famous mum. She's never ever ever come for you,' said Justine.

'Oh yes she has!' I yelled. 'She's come for me lots of times. She's going to come and take me away for good, we're going to Hollywood together and – will you stop *laughing* at me, you great big pig.'

'You're so stupid,' Justine gasped. 'Your mum's not a film star. Louise told me about your mum. She's nothing. And she's never coming for you. She hasn't been near you since you were little. I bet she's forgotten all about you. Or she's had heaps of other kids and doesn't want to think about that boring ugly Tracy ever again.'

So I hit her. And I kept on hitting her. And I don't care. I've made her nose bleed again. She's hurt me a bit too, but I don't care. And now I'm stuck in the Quiet Room and it's gone twelve and one of the other kids will get to go out to lunch with Cam instead of me and I don't care. At least it won't be Justine.

Maybe my mum *will* come.

There's someone outside the door. It's opening. *Is it Mum???*

No. It wasn't Mum. It never is. It was Cam, of course.

I took one look at Cam and burst into tears. Well, I would have done, if I was a crying sort of person.

'Oh dear,' said Cam. 'I don't seem to have a very good effect on you, Tracy.'

She sat right down on the floor beside me, waiting for me to quieten down a bit. Then she dug in the pocket of her jeans and found a crumpled tissue. She passed it to me and I mopped up my hay fever.

'Now,' said Cam. 'What do you want to do?'

'I haven't got any choice, have I? I'm stuck here.'

'No you're not. You can still come out to lunch with me. I've asked Jenny. Elaine explained why you got upset.'

'She doesn't know! I hate the idea of you lot all blabbing away about me,' I said fiercely.

'Yes, it must get a bit annoying,' said Cam. 'Still, at least it means you're the centre of everyone's attention. Here, you've still got a runny nose. Good job you weren't wearing your make-up this time.'

'Are you laughing at me?'

'Just a little tease. Coming?'

'You bet.'

Only I *still* felt bothered about my mum, even though I knew it was silly. I knew she almost definitely wouldn't be coming. I knew deep deep down that Justine was maybe right about her. But I still worried.

'My mum,' I mumbled.

'You're scared she'll come and you won't be here?' said Cam. 'OK. Tell you what we'll do. You can phone home when we're out. To check she's not arrived. And if she *has* I'll whisk you straight back. How about that?'

'That sounds great,' I said.

So Cam and I went off together for our lunch appointment after all. She's got this ancient grass-green Citroën which made a bit of a change from the Minivan.

'My mum wouldn't be seen dead in this sort of naff car,' I said. 'She drives a Cadillac you know.'

'Mm,' said Cam.

I squinted at her. 'You're just nodding to be nice to me aren't you?' I said. 'You don't really believe my mum's got her own Cadillac.'

Cam looked at me. 'Do you believe it, Tracy?'

I thought for a bit. 'Sometimes.'

Cam nodded again.

'And sometimes I know I'm sort of making it up,' I mumbled. 'Do you mind that? Me telling lies?'

'I make things up all the time when I write stories. I don't mind a bit,' said Cam.

'I've got that article with me. I've written it all. You won't have to bother with a thing. Shall I read a bit to you? You'll be really impressed, I bet you will. I think I've done a dead professional job.'

So I started reading it to her.

'You can see the signs of suffering on little Tracy Beaker's elfin face. This very very intelligent and extremely pretty little girl has been grievously treated when in so-called Care. Her lovely talented young mother had to put her in a home through no fault of her own, and in fact she might soon be coming for her lovely little daughter, but until then dear little Tracy Beaker needs a foster family. She is deprived and abused in the dump of a children's home— Why are you laughing, Cam?'

'Abused?' Cam spluttered.

'Look at my hand. My knuckles. That's blood, you know.'

'Yes, and you got it bouncing your fist up and down on poor Justine's nose,' said Cam. 'You're the one who deprives and abuses all the others in your Home.'

'Yes, but if I put that no-one will want me, will they?'

'I don't know,' said Cam. 'If I were choosing, I'd maybe go for a really naughty girl. It might be fun.'

I looked at her. And went on looking at her. And my brain started going tick tick tick.

I was mildly distracted when we got a McDonald's. I ate a Big Mac and a large portion of French fries, and washed it down with a strawberry milkshake. So did Cam. Then she had a coffee and I had another milkshake. And then we sat back, stuffed. We both had to undo our belts a bit.

I got out my article again and showed her some more, but she got the giggles all over again.

'I'll give myself hiccups,' she said weakly. 'It's no use, Tracy. I think it's great, but they'll never print it. You can't say those sort of things.'

'What, that Tracy Beaker is brilliant and the best child ever? It's true!'

'Maybe! But you can't say all the other things,

141

about Justine and Louise and the rest.'

'But they're true too.'

'No, they're not true at all. I've met them. I like them. And you certainly can't say those things about Jenny and Mike and your social worker and all the others. You'd get sued for libel.'

'Well, you do better then,' I said huffily. 'What would you put?'

'I don't know. Maybe I don't want to do the article now anyway. I think I'd sooner stick to my stories, and blow the money.'

'That's not a very professional approach,' I said sternly. 'Maybe you ought to give up writing. Maybe you ought to do some job that gives you a whacking great allowance. Looking after someone. You get an allowance for that.'

Cam raised her eyebrows.

'I can barely look after myself,' she said.

'Well then. You need someone to look after you for a bit,' I said. 'Someone like me.'

'Tracy.' Cam looked me straight in the eye. 'No. Sorry, *I* can't foster you.'

'Yes, you can.'

'Stop it. We can't start this. I'm not in any position to foster you.'

'Yes you are. You don't need to be married, you know. Single women can foster kids easy-peasy.'

'I'm single and I want to stay single. No husband. And *no kids*.'

'Good. I hate other kids. Especially boring little babies. You won't ever get broody, will you, Cam?'

'No fear. Holding that little Wayne was enough to douse any maternal urges for ever,' said Cam.

'So it could be just you and me.'

'No!'

'Think about it.'

Cam laughed. 'You aren't half persistent, girl! OK, OK, I'll think about it. That's all. Right?'

'Right,' I say, and I tap her hand triumphantly. 'Can I phone home now? I sound like E.T., don't I? We've got through two videos of that already. So, can T.B. phone home? Only she doesn't have any change.'

Cam gave me ten pence and I went to the phone by the ladies and gave Jenny a buzz. My heart did thump a bit when I was waiting for her to answer. I felt a little bit sad when she told me that Mum hadn't come. Even though that was the answer I was really expecting.

But I had other things to fuss about now. I whizzed back to Cam.

'Well? Have you had your think? Is it OK? Will you take me on?' I asked eagerly.

143

'Hey, hey! I've got to think about this for ages and ages. And then I'm almost certain it's still going to be no.'

'*Almost* certain. But not absolutely one hundred percent.'

'Mm. What about you? Are you absolutely one hundred percent sure you'd like me to foster you?'

'Well. I'd sooner you were rich. And posh and that, so that I could get on in the world.'

'I think you'll get on in the world without my help, Tracy.'

'No, I need you, Cam.'

I looked straight at her. And she looked straight at me.

'We still hardly know each other,' she said.

'Well, if we lived together we would get to know each other, wouldn't we, Cam? Camilla. That sounds classier. I want my foster mum to sound dead classy.'

'Oh Tracy, give it a rest. Me, classy? And I told you, I can't stick Camilla. I used to get teased. And that's what my mum always called me.' She pulled a face.

I was shocked by her tone and her expression.

'Don't you . . . don't you *like* your mum?' I said.

'Not much.'

'Why? Did she beat you up or something?'

'No! No, she just bossed me about. And my father too. They tried to make me just like them and when I wanted to be different they couldn't accept it.'

'So don't you see them any more?'

'Not really. Just at Christmas.'

'Good, so they'll give me Christmas presents, won't they, if I'm their foster grandchild?'

'Tracy! Look, it really wouldn't work. It wouldn't work for heaps of practical reasons, let alone anything else. I haven't got room for you. I live in this tiny flat.'

'I'm quite small. I don't take up much space.'

'But my flat's really minute, you should see it.'

'Oh great! Can we go there now?'

'I didn't mean—' Cam began – but she laughed again. 'OK, we'll go round to my flat. Only I told Jenny I'd take you back to the Home after lunch.'

'T.B. can phone home again, can't she?'

'I suppose so. Tell Jenny I'll get you back by teatime.'

'Can't I come to tea with you too? Please?'

'Tell you what. We could pretend to be posh ladies just to please you and have afternoon tea. About four. Although I don't know how either of us could possibly eat another thing. And then I'll take you back to the Home by five. Right?'

145

'What about supper? And look, I could stay the night, we're allowed to do that, and I don't need pyjamas, I could sleep in my underwear, and I needn't bother about washing things, I often don't wash back at the Home—'

'Great! Well, if you ever lived with me – and I said *if*, Tracy – then you'd wash all right. Now don't carry on. Five. Back at the Home. That'll be quite enough for today.'

I decided to give in. I sometimes sense I can only push so far.

I phoned, and Cam spoke to Jenny for a bit too.

'T.B.'s phoned home twice now. Like E.T. Do you know what E.T. got?' I said hopefully. 'Smarties.'

'You'll be in the Sunday papers tomorrow, Tracy. THE GIRL WHOSE STOMACH EXPLODED,' said Cam.

But she bought me Smarties all the same. Not a little tube, a great big packet.

'Wow! Thanks,' I said, tucking in.

'They're not just for you. Take them back and share them with all the others.'

'Oh! I don't want to waste them.'

'You're to share them, greedyguts.'

'I don't mind sharing them with Peter. Or Maxy. Or the babies.'

'Share them with everybody. Including Justine.'

'Hmm!'

She stopped off at another shop too. A baker's. She made me wait outside. She came out carrying a cardboard box.

'Is that cakes for our tea?'

'Maybe.'

'Yum yum. I'm going to like living with you, Cam.'

'Stop it now. Look Tracy, I seem to have got a bit carried away. I like seeing you and I hope we can go out some other Saturdays—'

'Great! To McDonald's? Is that a promise?'

'That really is a promise. But about fostering . . . I'd hate you to build your hopes up, Tracy. Let's drop the subject now and just be friends, OK?'

'You could be my friend *and* my foster mum.'

'You're like a little dog with a bone. You just won't let go, will you?'

'Woof woof!'

I'm getting good at making her laugh. I like her. Quite a lot. Not as much as my mum, of course. But she'll do, until my mum comes to get me.

Her flat came as a bit of a shock, mind you. It really is weeny. And ever so shabby. It's in far worse nick than the Home. And you should see her bedroom. She leaves her pyjamas on the floor too!

Still, once I get to live there I'll get her sorted out. Help her make a few improvements.

'Show me your books then,' I said, going over to the shelves. 'Did you write all this lot?'

'No, no! Just the ones on the bottom shelf. I don't think you'll find them very exciting, Tracy.'

She was dead right there. I flicked through one, but I couldn't find any pictures, or any funny bits, or even any rude bits. I'll have to get her to write some better books or she'll never make enough money to keep me in the style to which I want to become accustomed.

Maybe I'll have to hurry up and get my own writing published. I got Cam to give me a good long go on her typewriter.

It took me a while to get the hang of it. But eventually I managed to tap out a proper letter. I left it tucked away on Cam's desk for her to find later.

```
    DEAR CAM, I WILL BE THE BESTEST FOSTER
CHILD EVER. YOU'LL SEE. WITH LOVE FROM
TRACY BEAKER, THE GIRL WHOSE STOMACH DIDN'T
EXPLODE.
```

It did nearly though. Guess what she bought for tea! A birthday cake, quite a big one, with jam and cream inside. The top was just plain

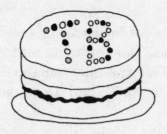

white, but she took some of my Smarties and spelt out T.B. on the top.

'So that it's all my cake,' I said happily.

'Aren't I going to get a slice?' asked Cam.

'Oh yes. Of course. But I don't have to share it with anyone else. I had to share my proper birthday cake with Peter, wasn't that *mean*!'

'I thought Peter's your friend.'

'Well. He is. But still. You don't want to share your birthday cake even with your bestest friend ever,' I said.

Only I started thinking about it all the time I was chomping my way through my first great big slice. And my second slice with extra jam and cream. And my third weeny slice. And my nibbles at a bit of icing.

'This is much better than that birthday cake at the Home, you know,' I said.

'Good.'

'Peter's gone out with this dumb sounding old auntie and uncle today,' I said.

'Has he?'

'But I bet they won't take him to McDonald's.

Or buy him his own special cake.'

'Maybe not.'

'Well, seeing as we are friends, Peter and me, and we share a birthday, and we shared that other birthday cake – maybe we *ought* to share this one too,' I said. 'Shall I take a slice back for my friend Peter?'

'I think that would be a good idea,' said Cam. 'I'll wrap up a slice for Peter. And another slice for you. Just so long as you promise me you won't throw up all night.'

'Of course I won't. Here, can I do the cutting this time? Because if this is like a birthday cake I get a wish, don't I?'

So Cam gave me the knife and I closed my eyes and wished really really hard.

'I bet you can't guess what I wished,' I said to Cam.

'I bet I can,' said Cam.

'I'll tell you if you like.'

'Oh no. You're supposed to keep birthday cake wishes secret,' said Cam.

I pulled a little face at her. Then I thought.

'Here, if this is a sort of birthday, then it's a pity there aren't any presents too.' I paused. 'Hint hint hint.'

'Do you know what you are, Tracy Beaker? Absolutely shameless.'

But it worked!

Cam looked all round her room and stared for a while at her bookshelves. I thought I was going to end up with a boring old book. But it was much much better. She went to her desk and picked up her Mickey Mouse pen.

'Here we are, Tracy. Happy Unbirthday,' she said, and she pressed the pen into my hand.

Just for a moment I was lost for words. And that doesn't happen very often to me. I was scared I might even get another attack of my hay fever. But I managed to grin and give her the thumbs up sign and show her that I was ever so pleased.

We got back to the Home at five. On the dot.

Trust her to be punctual at the wrong time. I made a bit of a fuss on the doorstep. I sort of clung a bit. It was just that I was enjoying myself so much that I wanted to go *on* enjoying myself. That's not being difficult, is it?

But it's still OK. She's coming next Saturday. She's promised. Twelve o'clock. We have a date, me and my future foster mum. I'm going to make that wish come true.

It took me a bit of time to calm down after we'd said goodbye. I missed out on tea, but it didn't really matter, seeing as I'd had more than half my cake and the McDonald's lunch and the Smarties. There were still quite a few Smarties left. Just no red ones. Or pink or mauve or blue. They're my favourite colours. But there were plenty of the boring ones to share with the others.

When I came out of the Quiet Room I collected my Smarties and the two slices of cake. They'd got a bit squashed as I was saying goodbye to Cam, but Jenny helped me spruce them up a bit and put them on a plate.

I went to find Peter. He was up in his room, sitting on his bed, looking a bit quiet.

'Oh oh,' I said. 'This older couple. They didn't turn up?'

'Oh yes. They did,' said Peter.

'But they were pretty awful, yes? Never you mind, Pete, see what I've got for us? Look, really yummy cake.'

'Thank you, Tracy,' said Peter, and he took his slice absent-mindedly. 'No, they aren't awful, Auntie Vi and Uncle Stanley. They're nice, actually.'

'I bet they didn't take you to McDonald's.'

'No, we went and had fish and chips. My nan and I always used to go and have fish and chips. With bread and butter and a cup of tea.'

'Boring! I had a Big Mac and French fries and a strawberry milkshake, two actually, and then Cam bought me these Smarties and then she bought me this really incredible cake and even put my name on the top. It was my extra special cake and I could have eaten it all up myself but I asked her to save a big slice for you. So I did. And you haven't even started on it yet. Don't you like it? It was meant to be your big treat.'

'Oh, it's lovely, Tracy,' said Peter, munching politely. 'It's ever so good of you. I told Auntie Vi and Uncle Stanley all about you and said that you were my best friend. They want to meet you very much.'

'Well, it's no use them getting interested in me. I'm going to be fostered by Cam, you wait and see.'

'Really? That's wonderful. You see, I think Auntie Vi and Uncle Stanley want to foster me, Tracy. That's what they said. They want to take me almost straight away.'

'So you're zooming off and leaving me in this dump, are you?' I said. 'Terrific!'

'Well. I don't *want* to leave you, Tracy. I told them that. But if you're going to be fostered too . . .'

'Yeah, yeah, well Cam's desperate to have me, but you shouldn't always rush into these things you know, Peter. You should think it over carefully.'

'I know. That's what I've been trying to do,' said Peter. 'Tracy. No matter who fosters me, who fosters you, we can still stay best friends, can't we? And visit each other lots? And write letters?'

'I'll write you letters with my very own special Mickey Mouse pen. Want to see it?'

'Oh, Tracy, you didn't nick it from Cam, did you?'

'Cheek! What do you take me for? She gave it to me, dumbo. I told you she's dotty about me. OK, We'll make a pact. We'll stay best friends no matter what. Here, you're leaving all the icing. Don't you like it?'

'Well, I was saving the best bit till last. But you have it, Tracy. I want you to have it, really.'

It's quite good, sharing a cake with your best friend.

Then I went round the whole Home with the packet of Smarties. I gave one each to everyone. I even gave one to Louise and the new girl. They were upstairs together, trying on the new girl's clothes.

Justine was downstairs. At the window. Her dad hadn't turned up. She had a new sticking plaster on her face. She was sniffling.

I looked at her. My heart started going thump thump thump. I went up to her. She turned round, looking all hopeful. She thought I was Louise. But it looks like Louise might have a new best friend now. Louise is like that.

Justine jumped a bit when she saw it was me.

'What do you want, Tracy Beaker?' she mumbled, wiping her eyes.

'I've got something for you, Justine,' I said.

I thought I was going to give her a Smartie. But you'll never guess what I did. I gave her my Mickey Mouse pen.

I must be stark staring bonkers. I hope Cam can get me another one. Next Saturday. When I see her. When she tells me that she's thought it all over and she wants to be my foster mum.

This started like a fairy story. And it's going to finish like one too. Happily Ever After.

Jacqueline Wilson

Tracy Beaker's Thumping Heart

Illustrated by Nick Sharratt

CORGI YEARLING

To Dr Sion Gibby
Dr Arvind Vasudeva
Dr John Foran
and all the staff at
St Anthony's Hospital and
the Royal Brompton Hospital
who looked after my own
thumping heart.

Tracy Beaker's Thumping Heart

It all started on St Valentine's Day. I'd never bothered about February 14th before. I don't go in for all that lovey-dovey slop. I certainly don't go a bundle on those sentimental satin hearts and huggy teddies and fat pink Cupid babies with wings. I'm Tracy Beaker, OK? Enough said.

The Dumping Ground

I live in a Dumping Ground. It's actually a Children's Home for looked-after kids. Ha. You only end up here if you're *not* looked after. It isn't a home at all. It's definitely a dump.

I'm only there on a temporary basis of course. My mum's coming for me soon, just you wait and see.

161

I know she misses me every bit as much as I miss her. It's just that she's otherwise engaged, holed up in Hollywood, making movies. She really is. Justine-Know-Nothing-Littlewood says I'm making it all up but you don't want to take any notice of *her*.

I just have to flash my special photo of my mum and it's perfectly obvious she's a film star. She's got lovely blonde wavy hair and big blue eyes and shiny pink lips. She's the prettiest woman I've ever seen in my life. Even Justine-Argy-Bargy-Littlewood doesn't dispute that.

'So how come she's got such an ugly little squirt for a daughter?' Justine said, jabbing at the photo, poking the baby Tracy right in the tummy. I'm in my mum's arms, cuddling up to her. I look cute as a button, all smiles, with tiny tufts on the top of my head. I'm not quite as cute nowadays. I generally glare rather than grin and my curls have exploded all over so that I

resemble a fuzzy floor mop. However, I am still *much* better looking than Justine-Bulgy-Eyed-Bullfrog-Littlewood. I might not be a Raving Beauty but I have Character. People say this all the time. I once had a social worker who was forever calling me a Right Little Character.

Elaine the Pain

I'm not sure how my current social worker Elaine the Pain would refer to me. I would possibly have to Delete some Expletives. I have an amazing vocabulary and often use long words. Expletives are *rude* words. (I often use them too!)

I won't need a social worker when my mum puts in an appearance, obviously. I expect this will be VERY SOON, the moment she's finished her mega movie commitments. Those Hollywood moguls are certainly keeping her busy as she hasn't written to me for *ages*.

I've got Mike and Jenny, who work at the Dumping Ground, on red alert for any phone calls from my mum. I often ask if she's phoned. Every day. Sometimes two or three times. They always sigh and say, 'No, sorry, Tracy' in this exasperated way. Exasperated is a posh word.

NO, SORRY, TRACY

163

It means people getting fed up with me. Folk are frequently exasperated when they deal with me.

It's not *my* fault. If only they wouldn't be so mean and give me my own mobile then I could make my own phone calls, no problem. A mobile is a bare necessity of modern life, for goodness' sake. I think it's outrageous that none of us kids in the Dumping Ground are allowed one until we're officially teenage, and even then it's a bog-standard pay-as-you-go embarrassment. Even Adele is limited to this type of manky mobile, and she's the oldest and coolest girl in the Dumping Ground. She's going to get her own flat soon. She's forever making plans for how she's going to furnish it and what she's going to do there.

'It's going to be Party Time every night of the week!' she says.

I hope she invites me to her parties. Adele is my favourite at the Dumping Ground. We hang out together lots. OK, she gets a bit Exasperated – with a capital E – when I experiment with her make-up and try walking in her amazing high heels.

She has been known to say, 'Jolly well clear off, Tracy Blooming Beaker' – or expletive words to that effect.

She's only kidding. She totally appreciates my company. In fact she frequently begs me to be her best friend. I might capitulate. (*Very* posh word for give in.) I very very rarely capitulate. I am one tough cookie who knows her own mind.

I *used* to be best friends with Louise. She's the prettiest kid here, with big blue eyes and long fair curls. She's *almost* as pretty as my mum. She looks as sweet as sugar but she's actually as sharp as knives. We used to have such fun together until Justine-Poach-My-Pal-Littlewood came along and stole her away from me.

Of course I could always get Louise back again as my best friend, easy peasy. But she's lost her chance. I don't *want* her now.

Adele is much more fun. Lots of people think so too. This was *abundantly* obvious on Saturday morning, Valentine's Day . . .

We were all sitting having our breakfast at the long table in the kitchen. The little kids were all strapped into their highchairs at one end, waving their soggy rusks and spooning up their mashed banana.

Maxy was kept up that end too. He's big enough to sit on a bench with us but you need to keep *way*

clear of him when he tucks into his cornflakes and slurps his orange juice. He doesn't just *spill*. He's such a greedy little beggar he gollops it all down too quickly, chokes, and then spurts it all out like a fountain – *not* a pretty sight.

The rest of us kids with passable table manners cluster together. I always used to sit beside Louise but now Justine-Jabbing-Elbows-Littlewood does her best to make me unwelcome. I generally sit next to Adele – and weedy Peter nudges up to my other side more often than not.

I haven't mentioned Peter up till now, though he actually plays an important part in this story. This is surprising because if you saw a photo of all of us kids in the Dumping Ground you'd find him the least significant. He's this weird little geeky kid with big eyes like Bambi and arms and legs as spindly as spaghetti.

He's always clutching a soggy lacy hankie in his little paw. It used to belong to his nan who looked after him until she died and little Pete got dumped alongside us. He hangs on to it like it's his cuddle blanket. It's soggy because he's frequently in tears. He's much too old for all his namby-pamby snuffles. He might only look about six but he's my age. *Exactly* my age. He has the cheek to have the same birthday as me so we have to share a birthday cake between us. We might share our star sign but we have NOTHING in common.

I never cry. I didn't even cry when Louise went off with Justine and they stole my totally private diary and wrote ludicrous lies all over it. I didn't so much as whimper when my mum forgot to send me a present last birthday. Correction: of course she sent me a present. Loads of them. A karaoke kit for definite. And maybe my own mobile, and a little laptop and an iPod and a genuine cowboy hat and new football boots, all sorts of stuff, but they somehow got lost in the post, stolen before I could lay my hands on my parcels. But I *still* didn't cry. I might have the odd attack of hayfever which everyone knows makes your eyes stream – but I never cry.

'I know you don't ever cry, Tracy,' says Peter. 'You are *soooo* brave.'

He isn't taking the micky. He idiolizes me. This is somewhat irritating. He trots round after me and hangs on my every word, no matter what. I don't

167

want him acting like my little shadow. I frequently tell him to shove off. But then his little white face crumples up and he has to mop his big eyes with his Nanny rag. This is an infuriating ploy. It makes you feel mean and then you have to be sweet to him to stop him blabbing. I'll offer him a bite of my Mars bar or I'll teach him a new naughty word or if I'm *really* feeling kind I'll tickle him under his scrawny little arms. He'll nibble at the Mars and gasp at the rude word and squeal when he's tickled and tell me that I'm the best kid in the Dumping Ground. In our town, in our county, in our country, in our world, in our own ultra-extensive universe.

I just nod and go, 'Yeah yeah yeah' because I know this already. I'm Tracy Beaker, right?

So Peter was sitting next to me at breakfast on the fourteenth. He nudged up so close he was practically sitting in my lap.

'Give us a bit of elbow room, Peter,' I said, giving him a shove.

'Sorry, Tracy,' he said, but he wriggled even closer so that his mouth was right next to my ear. 'I want to ask you something,' he said, his whisper tickling terribly inside my ear.

'What?' I said loudly, rubbing my ear.

'Sh! It's a secret,' said Peter.

I sighed. Peter was forever telling me secrets and they weren't very exciting. He'd confide enormously embarrassing stuff, like he sometimes wet the bed at night, as if he imagined this wasn't obvious to everyone, seeing as he wandered round the Home half the night trailing damp sheets like a waterlogged ghost.

'Tracy, it's the fourteenth of February today,' Peter whispered.

'That's not a secret,' I said.

'It's Valentine's Day,' Peter persisted.

'That's not a secret *either*,' I said, exasperated.

'Tracy, will you be my Valentine sweetheart?' Peter whispered.

'What? Oh yuck, Pete, I don't believe in all that sentimental slush,' I said.

'*I* do,' said Peter. 'Oh, Tracy, please say you will.'

He blinked at me with his big Bambi eyes. Justine-Big-Nose-Littlewood was peering in our direction, looking inquisitive.

'OK, but shut up about it now, right?' I hissed.

'So that's a yes?' said Peter, kicking his legs jubilantly under the table. He just happened quite by wondrous chance to kick Justine-Daddy-Long-Legs-Littlewood right in the shins!

'Ouch!' Justine shrieked.

169

'Well *done*, Peter,' I said. I gave him such a congratulatory clap on the back he nearly shot across the table top. Maxy stopped slurping cornflakes and shrieked with delight. He choked, with predictable results.

'Simmer down, kids,' said Jenny. 'This is worse than feeding time at the zoo.'

'Yeah, yeah, me a wild animal,' said Maxy, scratching himself vigorously and snatching a plate of mashed banana from one of the babies, who started howling.

'Behave, you lot!' said Mike, wielding his big wooden spoon, pretending to rap all our knuckles.

There was another rap at the front door, an important official rat-a-tat-tat. I felt a familiar clutch at my chest. I always wondered if it could possibly be my mum come calling for me at long last. All the noise of the room faded and I just heard the thump thump thump of my heart. Then Jenny came back into the kitchen with a huge pile of post in her arms.

'It was the postie,' she said. 'Hey guys, Valentine's cards!'

The babies went on spooning their banana, Maxy elaborated on his animal

170

imitation, but the rest of us sat upright, twitching. I suddenly *got* it. It was a competition. Who was going to get the most Valentine's cards???

Jenny was sorting through them all, giggling, especially when she found a card addressed to herself. Mike had a card as well, a big funny one that played a silly tune when he opened it up.

I stared at the rest of the cards in Jenny's hands. She doled them out. One for Justine-Absolutely-Ugly-Littlewood!!! Who on *earth* would send a Valentine's card to her? She seemed thrilled with it too, reading the dumb verse over and over and stroking the glittering silver heart on the front.

'Who's it *from*, Justine?' Louise asked. 'I didn't know you had a boyfriend! What's his *name*? Look, he's signed it!'

'I'm not telling. It's a secret,' said Justine-Smug-Git-Littlewood, clapping her card to her chest.

'You haven't got a boyfriend, not unless he's blind and stupid,' I said fiercely. 'I bet you sent that card to yourself!'

'No, I didn't, Sour-Grapes-Nobody-Loves-You-Beaker,' said Justine-Smug-Bug-Littlewood.

'Take no notice, Tracy,' Peter whispered right in my ear. 'She's talking rubbish. *I* love you. I'll make you a special Valentine's card.'

171

I couldn't concentrate on Peter and his tickly whisper and his offer of a crayoned card. I reached right over the table and snatched Justine's card. I only saw it for a second before she snatched it back, acting outraged, but it was enough time to read the message and the signature. It wasn't from a boyfriend at all. The card said *To dear Justine, Happy Valentine's Day, Love from Dad.*

I felt as if I'd been stabbed in the stomach. It was much much better than a card from a stupid boyfriend. I didn't even *have* a dad. Not that I cared. I had a mum and she was all that mattered to me. Had *she* sent me a Valentine's card?

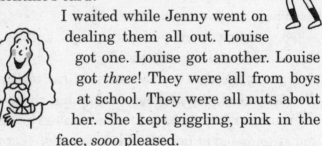

I waited while Jenny went on dealing them all out. Louise got one. Louise got another. Louise got *three*! They were all from boys at school. They were all nuts about her. She kept giggling, pink in the face, *sooo* pleased.

'Hey, Louise has got *three* valentines, look!' crowed Justine-Brag-A-Lot-Littlewood. 'Louise has got more Valentines than anyone else. So that proves she's the most popular girl here.'

'Not absolutely accurate,' said Adele, as Jenny gave her a *handful* of cards, one, two, three, four, *five* Valentines. The last was a huge one with a big red satin heart and a badge saying *Happy Valentine, Love you Lots, Babe*. Adele chuckled and pinned it on her top.

'Adele's got *five* Valentines, way more than anyone else in the whole Dumping Ground,' I said. 'So *she's* the most popular girl, right?'

'Adele doesn't properly count. She's not really a girl, she's nearly grown up, and she's got heaps of boyfriends anyway,' said Justine-Pedant-Littlewood. 'Louise got the most Valentines of all us kids. And I've got the prettiest Valentine because of all the silver glitter and the lovely verse. What have you got, Tracy Beaker? Absolute *zilch*.'

'That's all *you* know, Justine-Rubbish-Littlewood,' I said.

Jenny still had a few cards left. Maybe maybe maybe one was for *me*. If Justine's dad had sent her a card maybe my mum *might* just have decided to send me a Valentine. It would be a cool way for her to keep in touch. Maybe she'd write a special message: *To my darling little Tracy, Happy Valentine's Day, See you Very Soon, Lots of love, Mum.*

Jenny kept handing out the cards. She held up the last one, giggling, because it was another one addressed to *her*.

'Don't look so desperate, Tracy Beaker. Look, she's nearly in tears. Boo-hoo baby. Fancy getting in such a stupid state. No one would ever dream of sending *you* a Valentine,' said Justine Asking-For-A-Punch-Littlewood.

'That's just where you're wrong,' I said. I spoke slightly indistinctly.

'Absolutely one hundred percent wrong,' said Peter. 'I happen to know Tracy will be getting an enormous and very special card as soon as possible.'

'We don't count scribbly home-made efforts from little weeds,' said Justine-Crushing-Littlewood.

'She's not just getting a card, she's getting a Valentine's *present*!' Peter declared. 'She's getting it right this minute. Just you wait till you see what it is.'

He jumped off the bench and ran out of the room. Justine and Louise tittered together, while Mike went, 'Aaaah!' and Jenny went, 'Sweet!'

'I bet that's what he's going to give her – a sweet,' said Justine-Scoffing-Littlewood. 'He'll have probably sucked it first!'

Peter came charging back, carrying *something* in a tremendously sellotaped brown paper bag.

174

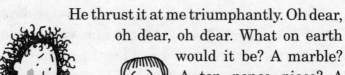

He thrust it at me triumphantly. Oh dear, oh dear, oh dear. What on earth would it be? A marble? A ten pence piece? A pebble with a message scratched in biro?

I knew just how much Justine would jeer.

'I think I'll open my parcel in private,' I said, simply trying to save Peter's feelings.

'No, no, open it *now*,' said Peter. 'You wait and see, Justine. Tracy's got a *fabulous* Valentine's present.'

'So you're giving her a Valentine's present, are you, little Petey-Wetey-Wet-The-Bed. Ah, how touching!' said Justine-Viper-Tongue-Littlewood.

Peter's white face flushed raspberry red.

'I *don't* wet the bed, Justine. And anyway, even if I did, Jenny says it's nothing at all to be ashamed of,' said Peter.

'Absolutely spot on, Peter,' said Jenny, her nose still inside her Valentine's cards. 'Come on, Tracy, open your present. We're all dying to see what it is.'

I could see there was absolutely no way I could sneak off and open Peter's wretched parcel in

175

private. I decided to brazen it out. If Justine dared sneer I'd pick up Maxy, shoogle him violently up and down and then aim him in her direction.

I struggled with my bitten nails to prise back the sellotape. It looked as if I might need bolt-cutters. I improvised, biting my way in. I peeled back layers of crumpled tissues – and stared at Peter's Valentine's present.

'What is it, then? Let us see!' said Justine-Long-Nosed-Littlewood.

 I silently held it up. It was a beautiful gold locket in the shape of a heart. Real gold. The heart was huge, almost as big as my fist. A gold heart like that must be worth hundreds and hundreds of pounds! Everyone gasped.

'Where on earth did you get *that*, Peter? You didn't nick it, did you?' said Louise.

'Don't be ridiculous, Louise,' said Jenny. She looked astounded too. 'Where *did* you get the locket from, Peter?' she asked.

'I've kept it hidden in a sock ever since I came here. It was my nan's,' said Peter. He said it proudly but his eyes filled with tears. He nearly always cried when he talked about his nan. 'She used to wear it on Sundays. It had a chain to match but I'm afraid it got broken. But the locket's still fine. Look, Tracy, you just press this little catch, see.'

He demonstrated with his small finger and the locket opened. There was a photo of an infant inside, a pale baby with little downy curls, big Bambi eyes, sticking out ears and a very skinny neck.

'That's me,' Peter said unnecessarily. He edged up to me again, whispering so the others wouldn't hear. 'Nan used to say I was her little sweetheart. Now I'm  your Valentine sweetheart, aren't I, Tracy?'

I didn't know what to say. I remembered the time Mike and Jenny took all us kids to a theme park and I went on the rollercoaster. My stomach felt exactly the same now. I was touched that weedy little Peter liked me enough to give me his nan's incredibly valuable locket – but all that sentimental sweetheart stuff made me want to throw up.

'What do you *say*, Tracy?' Mike prompted me.

I still couldn't speak. I held the gold locket tight in my hand and stared hard at the table top, praying that I wasn't about to succumb to an inconvenient bout of hayfever.

Jenny put her arm round Peter.

'It's such a sweet romantic gesture, Peter, but are you really sure you want to give your nan's very special heart to Tracy?'

'Of course he's sure!' I said indignantly.

'Maybe you could give Tracy the heart just for today?' Jenny persisted.

'What kind of a rum deal is that?' I said. 'Presents are meant to be *permanent*.'

'I want to give Tracy the heart for ever and ever,' said Peter fervently.

Justine-Has-To-Mock-Littlewood made silly whistling noises, rolling her eyes. Louise and the other kids copied her – but Adele smiled.

'Aah, you're such a little gent, Pete,' she said. 'You're a very lucky girl, Tracy.'

I nodded, clutching my gold heart.

'Now you'll have to find a very special place to keep your heart, Tracy,' said Jenny. 'It must be *very* valuable. I think I'd better pop it in the safe for the moment.'

'No way! I'm wearing it!' I said.

'For goodness' sake, Tracy, you're the girl who's always losing everything,' said Jenny. 'This week it was your pen, last week your swimming kit – and didn't we have to fork out for an entire new school bag for you last month? Of course I can't let you wear a real gold locket. Anyway, you haven't got a chain.'

'I'll *make* a special chain. Oh, Jenny, please, it means so much to me. No one's ever given me such a special incredibly expensive present – apart from my mum, of course,' I said, laying it on thick.

'Go on, Jenny, let her wear her locket!' said Mike.

'All right. You can wear it at the weekends, Tracy, so long as you look after it ultra-carefully. I haven't got the heart to argue with you any more. *Heart*, get it!'

I tittered obligingly and sauntered off to manufacture my chain. Peter skipped along beside me, beaming so brightly his lips nearly met at the back of his head.

'Do you really really really like your Valentine's locket, Tracy?' he burbled.

'Yes, I do. I'm going to wear it all the time, even at school. I'll get round Jenny somehow. I can't wait to show it off. It's so big! It must be worth a fortune!'

'Well, to be absolutely truthful it isn't really worth a fortune, Tracy. It isn't actually *gold* gold,' said Peter, looking very worried.

'What are you on about? Of *course* it's gold,' I said, holding the locket up.

'It's just gold-*coloured*, Tracy. My granddad won it for my nan at a fairground. You have to keep polishing it like crazy or it goes a sort of green colour – but I've made it lovely and shiny now. It *looks* like real gold. You don't mind that it isn't *actually* gold, do you, Tracy?'

179

I minded terribly. I'd never owned any real jewellery before. None of the kids in the Dumping Ground had *proper* jewellery. Adele had sparkly studs in her ears but they weren't real diamonds. Justine-Tacky-Littlewood and Louise just had yucky bead friendship bracelets.

I so wanted everyone to envy me having a real gold heart locket worth a fortune. They'd all laugh at me if they knew it was a trashy old fairground prize. I couldn't let them find out.

'To me it's real gold, Peter,' I said firmly, threading it on a piece of string.

It didn't have exactly the right effect. I sidled into Adele's room while she was in the bathroom and had a quick rummage through her dressing-table drawers. I came across just the job, a white broderie anglaise blouse threaded with thin red velvet ribbon. I wondered about asking . . . but Adele was still a bit narked because I'd dressed up in her black high heels to be a Spanish dancer and I'd stamped a little too vigorously and one of the silly heels fell off. She'd said I couldn't ever ever ever borrow her clothes again.

Oops!

I didn't want to borrow her whole blouse, just the red velvet ribbon running round it, but I still had a funny feeling she'd object. So I had one quick tug at the ribbon and suddenly there it was, in my hand.

I charged back to my room and tied it with the gold heart. It looked great! Oh dear, if only it were *real* solid gold and worth something!

'It looks lovely on you, Tracy,' said Peter.

'Yes, it does,' I said, smoothing the ribbon and stroking the heart.

'So we're really sweethearts now?' Peter said eagerly.

'If you say so,' I said.

'Oh, I do! I really love you, Tracy.'

He waited, his head on one side.

'Do you love me, Tracy?'

'Oh, *Pete*. Look, I'm not into all that dopey lovey-dovey stuff.'

He blinked his big Bambi eyes, his lip starting to tremble.

'Don't look so *stricken*! It's not *you*, Peter. It's not personal at all. I'm never going to fall in love. I'm Tracy Beaker. I'm *immune*.'

Little did I know that sneaky baby Cupid was lurking in a corner, arrow poised, about to pierce my heart.

I did a little tap dance downstairs, my gold heart bouncing on the end

 of the red ribbon. I paused at the window on the landing. You could see all the way down the drive to the gates at the end. I usually leant against this window and waited on Saturdays. I paused here today.

'Are you watching out for . . . anyone?' Peter asked delicately.

I nodded.

'I'll wait with you,' said Peter.

He didn't have anyone to watch for, not unless his own nan popped down a celestial ladder from heaven and shuffled up the drive in her Dr Scholl's. He was just keeping me company.

I was watching for my mum of course. She's going to come and see me very soon. I might just have mentioned this before. Justine-Relentlessly-Evil-Littlewood says my mum's forgotten all about me and isn't ever going to come and see me. But she is *sooo* wrong and if she says it again I'll punch her on the nose. Of course my mum's coming. Very very soon. On Saturday. That's what she said when I last saw her.

It was quite a long time ago but I remember every single second so very clearly. Mum took me out and we went for this incredibly posh meal. I couldn't *believe* the prices! It meant my mum thought the whole world of me. She let me order

182

absolutely everything I fancied on the menu, with a double portion of French fries and then *two* puddings and *then* lots of little chocolates on a pretty saucer.

It was the best meal I'd ever had. I didn't hang on to it for very long. I was so excited to see my Mum that my tummy went fizz fizz fizz and I had to gallop in double-quick time to the ladies' where I was horribly sick. Mum was a bit cross with me then and I don't blame her because she'd forked out a small fortune on that meal then I'd wasted it all. But she mopped me up and we went to buy me a new top because the one I was wearing got a bit splashed. It wasn't just an ordinary T-shirt from Primark – it was *designer*. Mum didn't flinch as she flashed her credit card.

Then Mum took me to the cinema. I so hoped it was going to be one of Mum's films and I'd see her acting at last, but it was a cartoon film. It had a fairy-tale princess in it, with long golden hair just like my mum though. And then Mum took me back

183

to the Dumping Ground and I had a very severe attack of hayfever.

Mum told me I mustn't make such a silly fuss, she'd come and get me for good as soon as she could get everything sorted, and meanwhile she'd visit me as often as possible.

'Next Saturday?' I said, and Mum said, 'Sure.' She even called, 'See you Saturday' as she waved and went down the drive.

So I waited. I thought she meant the actual *next* Saturday but she didn't come. Then I realized she meant *a* Saturday. So I wait for her every Saturday, watching from the window to get the first glimpse of her. I stand at the window and stare out, concentrating hard. I stare at the gates and will Mum to walk through them.

So I stared and stared and stared, and Peter stood beside me, staring too. Then I heard Adele shouting that *someone* had been in her room messing about with her clothes, and I felt a little too prominent in my window-watching position. I scooted downstairs, Peter at my side, and went into our sitting room. Maxy was watching television while still eating his breakfast toast. He was so absorbed watching some silly cartoon that he frequently missed his mouth, smearing butter all over his cheeks and chin.

184

'Tracy's my Valentine sweetheart,' Peter said.

Maxy grunted, unimpressed.

'I think you should be Justine's sweetheart, Maxy. The minute she comes downstairs run and give her a great big kiss. Rub your face all over her,' I said.

'Really?' Maxy said indistinctly.

'Absolutely,' I said, although Peter frowned at me.

'*Swap Shop's* starting on the other channel,' said Peter. 'Let's watch that instead. It's good, isn't it, Tracy?'

I shrugged. I didn't know any of the Saturday morning shows because of my weekly vigil on the stairs, but I'd heard some of the other kids talking about it. There was this funny furry little fox telling silly jokes, and there was some young guy presenter, Billy or Barry or . . . 'Hi, I'm Barney.'

 He was smiling straight out of the television – straight at *me*. His warm brown eyes shone and his cheeky face lit up. I loved his funny monkey T-shirt. He looked like a big brother who loved fooling around and making jokes – and yet he had big strong arms that could give you a hug, just like a dad.

There was a *twang* in the room as that pesky little Cupid shot his arrow, and a *thunk* as it

shot straight through my sweater and pierced my heart. Not Peter's nan's not-real-gold locket. My own red thumping heart pulsing inside my ribcage.

I sat down beside Maxy, even though I was risking getting a piece of chewed toast stuck in my ear. Peter sat neatly cross-legged on the other side of me.

'This is a good programme, Tracy,' he said. 'I love Basil Brush. And I like Barney too. Do you like him?'

'Yeah, he's OK,' I mumbled. Like! He was *fantastic*!

Barney smiled as if he could hear us.

'Who likes a hearty breakfast?' he asked, grinning, 'Cupid!'

I snorted with laughter.

'Did you get any Valentine cards today?' asked Barney. 'I didn't, sob sob.'

'I got hundreds!' said Basil Brush. 'I know a lot of foxy ladies – boom boom!'

Barney sighed and rolled his brown eyes. 'Here's a little Valentine verse just for you.'

He was looking straight at me!

'Roses are red,

Violets are blue,

Watch *Swap Shop* on Saturday

And I'll love you true.'

'I'll love *you*, Barney,' I said inside my head.

He nodded and gave me a wink. But our thrilling telepathy was suddenly obliterated by Justine-Foghorn-Littlewood barging into the room, shrieking with laughter over something stupid. Maxy hurled himself at her and nuzzled her neck romantically. He spread slime, snot and soggy toast all over her head, hair and sweater in a highly satisfactory fashion. She shrieked even louder.

Mike came running, convinced she was being murdered (I *wish*!). When he'd calmed her down he stayed to watch *Swap Shop* with us.

'I used to watch *Swap Shop* when *I* was a kid,' he said. 'And is that Basil Brush? He doesn't look quite the same. I'm sure his snout used to be more pointy. He looks a bit too cuddly now. Who's the scruffy guy with him? He used to be with Mr Derek.'

'Oh Mike, you are hopeless! That's Barney. Justine and I think he's seriously cool,' said Louise.

How dare they! He was *my* Barney!

'Yeah, we like his funky little bit of face-fuzz,' said Justine-Leery-Eyes-Littlewood, mopping herself with a J-cloth. 'Hey look, that girl wants to swap a karaoke kit for something else. Is she *mad*? I'd give anything for one. I'm going to phone in and offer to swap it for . . . What can I offer, Lou?'

'I could offer my hair-straightening kit now I've decided to go for the naturally curly look,' she said.

'I could swap my rubber Dumbo for it,' said Maxy.

'*You're* the Dumbo, Maxy! It's worth about five pence maximum after you've slobbered all over it,' said Justine-Spurn-Her-Sweetheart-Littlewood. 'You've got to swap something of equivalent value. A karaoke kit is worth *heaps*.'

'Do you want a karaoke kit, Tracy?' Peter said.

Of *course* I did. It would be so cool to plug it in and belt out a little number with proper musical accompaniment. Maybe I could even croon a ballad for Barney! Only what could I swap? My possessions were as manky as Maxy's. All my books were wrinkly because I read them in the bath. My skateboard buckled that time I played dodgem dustbins. My CD player broke when I dropped it down the stairs. I'd lost my left flashing trainer and my right footie boot and *both* my rollerblades. I didn't have anything – and yet I *so* wanted a karaoke machine.

I was sure I could sing better than the stars. It would be my chance to be discovered. Forget Amy, forget Lily. You're toast, Rhianna and Duffy. Tracy Beaker, singing superstar, is taking to the stage.

My heart started thumping. I fingered my gold heart locket. It wasn't real gold but it looked like it. Jenny and Mike and all the other kids except Peter thought it was real gold and worth a fortune. Worth way more than a karaoke machine. But I couldn't swap Peter's heart . . . could I?

It wasn't Peter's any more though. He'd given it to me. I could legitimately do what I liked with it: keep it in my treasure box, wear it on a ribbon, sell it to a jeweller, *swap it* . . . And it wasn't as if it was *worth* anything.

Justine-Out-To-Outdo-Me-Littlewood was already begging Mike to lend her his mobile.

'Quick, quick, I need to get through to *Swap Shop now*, Mike. Louise and I are offering to swap her hair-straightening kit.'

'Are you OK with this, Louise?' said Mike. 'It's *your* hair-straightening do-da.'

'Yes, that's fine. Justine and I will share the karaoke machine,' said Louise.

'That's what best friends are for. Sharing!' said Justine-Snatch-*My*-Friend-Littlewood.

I felt as if she'd punched me in the chest. My heart thumped. I suddenly put my arm round Peter.

'*We're* best friends, aren't we, Pete?' I said.

'Oh *yes*, Tracy,' said Peter, his big eyes shining. 'Sweethearts *and* best friends.'

'We'd like to share a karaoke kit, wouldn't we?' I said.

Peter nodded a little less certainly.

'If only we had something brilliant to swap,' I said. 'Something worth much much more than a silly old hair-straightening kit. Can you think of anything, Peter?'

Peter blinked, looking bewildered.

'Quick, quick, Justine's phoning already. We *have* to outbid her!' I said urgently. 'Think, Pete, think! Have we got *anything*?'

190

I fingered the heart locket ostentatiously (meaning I practically thrust it in Peter's face). He gazed at it, a little cross-eyed.

'Well . . . all I can think of is my nan's heart locket,' he said.

'Yes! Yes, of course! Oh well done, Peter! You're sure you don't mind?' I gabbled, pulling him over towards Mike.

'Well, it's your heart locket now, Tracy. Don't *you* mind?' said Peter.

'Of course I mind. Very much,' I said. 'But we both know it isn't really worth anything. And it looks pretty but it doesn't really *do* anything, does it? Not like a karaoke machine. I'll let you have first go if we can swap it.'

'Hey, Tracy, what are you talking about?' said Mike. 'What are you saying to Peter? You're not saying you want to swap his nan's *heart*?'

'It's OK, it's not *real* gold, so it's not like it's really valuable – only *they're* not to know,' I hissed, and I grabbed the phone from Justine-Long-Winded-Littlewood.

'Give that back, I haven't finished!' she shrieked.

'You've *had* your turn. It's *mine* now,' I insisted. 'Isn't that right, Pete?'

'Hey hey hey!' said the guy at the end of the phone. 'Stop squabbling, you lot!'

'Is that *you*, Barney?' I said, hanging onto the phone, fingers superglued to the handset.

'No, sorry, I'm not Barney. Or Basil Brush either.'

'Boom boom!' I said.

'Exactly,' said the person. 'I'm Ben. I just work for the programme. Now, are you all one family? I've got Justine's name down – and Louise too. Are they your sisters?'

'NO WAY!' I said. 'Take no notice of their pathetic offering. Whoever wants a boring old hair-straightening kit?'

'You certainly *need* one, Tracy Beaker. You look like your head's been plugged into a light socket,' yelled Justice-Big-Gob-Littlewood.

'Shut *up*, Justine,' I bellowed. 'This is my turn. Isn't it, Ben?' I said down the telephone.

'If you say so,' said Ben.

'I want to talk too!' said Maxy, grabbing for the phone with his revoltingly sticky paws.

'No, get *off*, Maxy! Yuck, you're getting slurp all over my skirt, stop it!'

'Are you watching *Swap Shop* with a whole bunch of friends?' said Ben.

'Do we *sound* like friends?' I asked, mega-exasperated. 'More like deadly enemies! We live in this Dumping Ground.'

'Tracy!' said Mike. 'Children's Home, *if* you please. And hurry up, that's my own personal phone and you're costing me a fortune.'

'I'm *trying* to hurry up,' I said. 'Listen, Ben, I've got this amazing gold locket. I just *know* that karaoke girl will want to swap for it.'

'Are you sure it's *your* gold heart locket, Tracy?' asked Ben. 'It's not your mum's?'

'Of course it's not my *mum's*. As if I'd want to swap it then!' I said. 'No, it's a long story. My friend Peter gave it to me, for Valentine's day, actually, but we both think a karaoke set would be *way* more exciting, don't we, Peter?'

I prodded him and he nodded, though his bottom lip was quivering for some reason.

'Well, if there's an interesting story attached to this heart maybe you and some of your friends – or deadly enemies – might like to come along to the *Swap Shop* studio next week. You could show off your gold locket, Tracy.'

'And I'll meet Barney?'

'You'll meet everyone – Melvyn, Basil Brush, Frosty the Snowman, Keith the swapping hamster – *and* Barney. I think it would be a great idea for all you guys to be in our skip full of kids. You and Peter and Justine and Louise and Maxy and any other of your pals in the Children's Home. You could try to swap a karaoke set for all of you. Tracy, you've gone very quiet. You're still there, aren't you?'

'Yes,' I said. 'Um, can you just run that past me again, Ben? You're saying I'm invited to the studio to meet Barney, and I'm going to be, like, on *television*? Me, Tracy Beaker?'

'*What?*' shrieked Justine-Totally-Jealous-Littlewood. 'Tracy Beaker's going to be on *Swap Shop*? That's not FAIR! It was all *my* idea. I phoned up first. *I* should be picked to go on television!'

'Pipe down you lot!' Mike bellowed. 'Would you mind handing me my phone, please? If *any* of you are appearing on television then *I* need to be involved. Shh, the lot of you!'

He talked long and earnestly, sometimes nodding, sometimes shaking

194

his head, while we listened, holding our breath.

'Well, thank you so much. I'll e-mail you all the details,' said Mike, and he switched off his phone.

We all started clamouring. He held up his arms for silence.

'OK kids, they want six of you there at the studios next week for the show. It's all fixed.'

'HURRAY! HURRAY! HURRAY!' we shrieked, jumping up and down.

Justine-Still-Not-My-Friend-Littlewood hugged Louise. I was so jubilant I hugged Maxy, rendering myself seriously sticky, in need of a thorough hosing down. I went to hug Peter too but he hung back, rubbing his cuddle hankie against his nose.

'What's up, Peter? Come on, be *happy*, we're going to be on television!' I said, giving him a little shake.

'I'm not sure I *want* to be on television,' he said in a tiny voice, muffled behind his hankie.

'Of course you do. Don't worry, you don't have to *say* anything. I'll say it all for you.'

'Yeah, Tracy-Big-Blabbermouth,' said Justine-She-Can-Talk-Littlewood.

'You can just shut up, Justine. I don't know why *you're* jumping up and down like a jackass because *you're* not going. Or you, Louise. *I'm* the one they invited. Me, Tracy Beaker. *I* get to choose my five companions. Get it?'

'Stop shouting, Tracy,' said Jenny, coming in from the kitchen with a baby on either hip. 'What were you all yelling about? What's going on, Mike?'

'The kids are going to be on *Swap Shop* on the telly next week,' said Mike, grinning.

'Oh no they're not,' said Jenny.

'Oh yes we *are*,' I said, sounding like we were doing a pantomime routine.

'No, Tracy. I'm sorry, you *can't* be on television. There are all sorts of regulations about looked-after children. We'd never get permission in time,' said Jenny.

'Look, my mum's quite probably coming to see me this very Saturday so we can get her permission today,' I said.

'Now, Tracy, I know you'd love to see your mum, but you know she isn't really coming,' Jenny said very quietly.

'Yes, she is so!'

'Tracy, we're not even very sure where she *is* at the moment,' said Jenny.

'She's in Hollywood, I keep *telling* you! Are you deaf or stupid?' I yelled, hating Jenny.

'Ha ha ha, Tracy Beaker. *You* can't go but *I* can, because I see my dad heaps and he'd be over the moon to watch me on television,' crowed Justine-Impossibly-Hateful-Littlewood.

'No, you're not any of you going. It's against the rules and would involve endless paperwork,' said Jenny.

'Look, I've said they can go and they're *going*,' said Mike. 'Any other kid in the country can go on telly so why can't they? I don't care if it gets us into trouble. I'm taking them and that's that.'

We all fell on Mike, giving him huge hugs.

But it was Jenny who battled with all the phone calls and paperwork. I passed by her office and saw her simultaneously typing an e-mail, talking on the phone and jiggling a whimpering baby on her lap.

The baby kept trying to hurl herself onto her head just to add to Jenny's problems.

'That baby thinks she's a lemming,' I said. 'Here, I'll take her, shall I?'

I scooped the baby up. She blinked at me in surprise and then reached eagerly for the gold heart round my neck.

'Naughty! I don't want your tiny teeth-marks all over it. It's my special swap for Saturday,' I said.

Jenny snorted and muttered a very rude word about *Swap Shop*.

'Um! I wouldn't half get told off if *I* said that. Jenny, I *can* go on *Swap Shop* can't I? I can't miss this huge big chance to star on television. I might get discovered, impress them so much they offer me my own kid's show. After all, acting's in my blood! Look at my mum, the famous Hollywood movie star.'

'Oh, Tracy,' said Jenny.

'She *is*,' I said. 'Just you wait, she'll be coming for me any day now.'

Jenny nodded wearily.

I waited, joggling the baby.

'Jenny . . .'

'Yes, Tracy.'

'You said you don't know where my mum is.'

'Mm.' Jenny reached out and stroked my arm. 'We've been trying to get in touch. Apparently she's moved on from her last known address.'

'Because she's in Hollywood. *Obviously*,' I said.

We looked at each other.

'Right,' said Jenny, sighing.

'Hey, hey, I told you no biting!' I said to the baby, who was drooling all over the heart.

'Tracy, about Peter's nan's locket—'

'It's *my* locket now.'

'Yes I know. But I don't think you realize that it's maybe very upsetting for Peter that you want to swap it straight away.'

'But it's not real gold. It's not worth anything, Jenny, I promise.'

'What about sentimental value?'

'You're talking to me, Tracy Beaker. I'm not into sentiment, Jenny,' I said briskly.

I did pursue the matter a little further with Peter though. I cornered him that night when we both had occasion to go to the linen cupboard for clean sheets.

'You're sure you're OK about me swapping my heart locket, Peter?' I said.

'Yes, that's fine, Tracy,' he said, snuffling into his nanny hankie.

'It'll be *sooo* great to have a karaoke machine, won't it?' I said. 'We'll sing a duet, you and me, Peter. That will be fun, won't it?'

'Yes, Tracy,' Peter mumbled.

I gently unhooked his hankie from his nose and prodded the corners of his mouth.

'Smile, then!'

He smiled obediently. So that was all right then.

He wasn't smiling early on Saturday morning. He was crying.

'Oh, for goodness' sake, Pete, what's *up* with you? This is our big day,' I said, giving him a little shake.

'I've-lost-my-hankie!' he sobbed.

'What? Oh, give me a break! Get a tissue from the bathroom.'

'No, it's my nan's hankie, it got mixed up in the sheets and they're all higgledy-piggledy in the laundry basket and I can't *find* it!' Peter wailed.

'I'm not sure I'd *want* to find it in amongst a load of damp smelly sheets!' I said. 'Oh, cheer up, Peter. I'm sure Jenny will find it for you, and if she doesn't she'll get you a brand new hankie.'

'I don't want a new hankie, I want my *old* hankie that belonged to my nan,' Peter wept.

200

'Now look! This is our big day. It means *sooo* much to me. I'm going to meet Barney and get a karaoke machine! So don't spoil it for me, OK?' I said.

Peter blinked at me, sniffling. 'I'm sorry, Tracy,' he squeaked. He tried to smile again, even though the tears were still streaming down his cheeks.

'You are such a *baby*, Peter,' said Justine-Utterly-Lacking-Compassion-Littlewood. 'Hey, Lou, do you think I look OK in this top or should I change it?'

'It's lovely, keep it on. But what about me?' said Louise. 'I'm not sure about wearing pink. Is it, like, *too* girly?'

'Excuse me!' I said. 'As if it matters. No one will be looking at you. *I'm* the one doing the swap. You'll just be in the background, *lurking*.'

'Pulling faces behind you,' said Justine-Can't-Ever-Be-Trusted-Littlewood.

'I can pull really scary faces, look,' said Maxy, pulling his eyelids down and his nose up, grinning like a gargoyle.

'You're seriously scary all the time, Maxy,' said Mike, pretending to cower away from him. 'Right, you guys, are we ready for the off? One, two, three, four, five . . . Where's Adele? Adele, come on!'

'I'll get her,' I said, charging up the stairs.

201

Melvyn

I was worried she'd changed her mind. She'd said she didn't want to go on a silly little kids' programme, thank you very much – but she gave into my pleading when she caught a glimpse of Barney's pal Melvyn on the television.

'He looks kind of cute,' she'd said. 'I love the way he does his hair. OK, Tracy, if it means all that much to you I'll come. *If* I feel like it on the day.'

'Adele, Adele, *please* feel like coming! You're my best friend. You jolly well have to support me,' I said now, barging into her room.

'Hey, hey, I'm just putting on my make-up,' said Adele.

She looked incredible: amazing outlined eyes, pearly lips, glitter on her cheeks, just like a fashion model.

'Oh, wow, you look wonderful. Can *I* have some make-up too, Adele? Please please please make me up to look like you,' I begged, although I was conscious of Mike downstairs bellowing at us to get a move on.

'You're not old enough for proper make-up, Tracy,' said Adele.

'Just a speck of lippy,' I pleaded.

'You're lippy enough already,' said Adele. 'How about a splodge of red lipstick on your nose – the

202

comic clown effect? It'll match your red velvet ribbon round your neck!' She scribbled scarlet on my nose. I shrieked – but she took her tissue and wiped it straight *off*.

'Come on, then, Tracy. You look fine just as you are, I promise,' said Adele, ruffling my corkscrew curls. She was staring at my customized locket chain. 'Why does that ribbon look weirdly familiar?'

I shrugged and rushed her downstairs hurriedly. Jenny and all the littlies waved us goodbye and wished us luck. We all climbed into the mini van and we were off.

There was a five minute squabble about who was sitting where, everyone trying to steer well clear of Maxy, though Jenny had attacked him with an entire packet of wet wipes. Mike distracted us with a sing-song, and most of us joined in, practising for when I had my karaoke kit. Peter didn't sing very loudly. His voice was just a little mouse squeak.

As we got nearer and nearer the studio I found my tummy went tight and all *I* could manage was a squeak. My heart was going thump thump thump. I was about to meet Barney and be on television and it was so exciting – but oh-so-scary too. What if Barney didn't take any notice of me? What if I couldn't think of anything to say? I leaned forward and mumbled something of the sort into Mike's ear.

'You can't *help* noticing you, Tracy. And I've never *ever* known you at a loss for words,' he said.

We arrived at the studio and Mike announced to the doorman that we were Tracy Beaker and Party.

I loved that.

'I'm Tracy Beaker and you are my party!' I sang.

'You're Tracy Beaker and you are so *farty*,' sang Justine-Very-Vulgar-Littlewood.

We all had to get signed in, me and my party, and then we were led to a *dressing room*. I wanted it to have TRACY BEAKER, SUPERSTAR! on the door, but it just had a plain old number. Still, it was a very swish room, with a big mirror and two stylish sofas.

'Of course, this is pretty bog-standard compared with my *mum's* dressing rooms,' I said. 'She has white velvet sofas. They give her a new spotless one each week. And there's a chandelier and a white rug so soft she sinks in it up to her ankles.'

No one seemed to be listening to me, not even Peter. He was sucking his thumb, his chin on his chest.

'For goodness sake, Pete, you'll fuse all the cameras if you go into the studios with a face like that,' I said. I gave him a little prod. I wanted him to prod me back. He didn't. He just bent over further, his knees buckling.

'Come here, little pal,' said Mike, putting his arm round him. 'Don't worry about the hankie, I'm sure Jenny will find it for you. Or we'll get you another special hankie.'

'There isn't another one. Not one that belonged to my

205

nan,' Peter mumbled around his thumb. 'It's all I've got left of her.'

Mike leaned over Peter's head, looking at me.

'Do you hear what he's saying, Tracy?' he said.

I didn't *want* to hear. My heart was still going thump thump thump. Then there was a knock on my dressing room door and there was *Barney*!

'It's really *you*, Barney!' I gasped.

'No, actually I'm a cardboard cut-out,' he said, laughing. 'Hi, you must be Tracy.'

He picked me out! He knew me as soon as our eyes met!

'How did you know I'm Tracy?' I asked, thrilled.

'Oh, you're just how I imagined. And maybe your heart locket gave me a little bit of a clue. Oh dear though, Tracy, it looks a very special gold locket. I'm not sure we can let you swap it if it's really valuable.'

'No, it's fine, Barney. It's not solid gold,' I said hastily. 'It isn't really worth much, is it, Peter?'

Peter shook his head, his thumb still stoppering his mouth.

'And we're desperate to get that karaoke kit, aren't we, Peter?' I said.

Peter nodded this time, still mute.

'Well, we'll do our best to get it for you, kids,' said Barney. 'I think we're ready for you in the studio now. Come and meet Melvyn and Basil.'

We trooped along behind him. I hopped and skipped until I was beside him, staring up at him smiling and smiling and smiling.

'Are you excited about being on television, Tracy?' said Barney.

'You bet I am,' I said. I tried fluttering my eyelashes at him.

'Have you got something in your eyes, sweetheart?' said Barney. 'Try blinking hard.'

It was blinking hard trying to concentrate. I couldn't take my eyes off Barney and his soft hair and his big brown eyes and the little fuzzy down on his upper lip. My heart ached where the arrow had struck.

We trooped into the studio and stepped over snaky cables to the brightly coloured set. There were guys dressed up as lions and tigers and bears, a big Frosty the Snowman, children milling around, and a huge tank full of lime green gunge.

'A swimming pool!' Maxy yelled, hurtling towards it.

Mike managed to rugby-tackle him just as he was about to dive straight in.

'He's a game little chap,' said Barney, chuckling. 'But what's up with you, little guy?' He bent down to talk to Peter. 'Why are you all droopy-poopy? Don't you want to be on television?'

'*Tracy* wants to be on television,' Peter mumbled.

'And do you do what Tracy says, eh?' said Barney. 'Is she the boss?'

'She's not *my* boss,' said Justine-Can't-Bear-To-Be-Ignored-Littlewood.

'Tracy *is* a bit bossy,' said Peter. 'But I don't mind. She's my sweetheart.'

'Aah!' said Barney.

'I'm his sweetheart but he's not *mine*,' I whispered into Barney's ear.

Barney nodded though he didn't look as if he absolutely understood. But there was no time to elaborate as we were being prodded into position for the start of the show. I had to sit on a special chair beside Barney and Basil Brush popped up beside him.

'Oooh! It's a little doggy!' yelled Maxy.

'I am not a *dog*, little boy,' said Basil Brush, giving him a poke with his pointy snout. 'Why did the dog kennel leak, humm? It needed a new *woof*! Boom Boom!'

'Silly doggy,' said Maxy, unimpressed.

'Quit being a pain, Maxy,' said Justine-Interfering-Littlewood.

She stood right behind my chair, and when

I peered round at her she was pouting at the camera in sick-making fashion. Louise was simpering too and Adele was striking a pose, hand on her hip.

Peter was standing a little apart. He reached for the bottom of his sweater and held it awkwardly up to his nose, rubbing against it. He was so hopelessly lost without his nan's hankie. It was all he had left of her. Apart from the heart locket . . .

My own heart went thump thump thump.

'We're on air in ten seconds,' said Barney. 'Good luck, kids.'

My heart was thumping so hard I thought it would burst right out my sweater. The *Swap Shop* music started and Barney and Basil chatted away, welcoming everyone to the show.

'We're particularly delighted to welcome Tracy here, with all her friends—'

'And enemies,' muttered Justine-Can't-Shut-Up-Littlewood.

'—who live in a Children's Home and very much want a karaoke machine to have fun with,' said Barney. 'So what have you got to swap, Tracy?'

'I've got this very special unique gold locket,' I said, holding it up.

'And who gave it to you?' said Barney.

'My friend Peter gave it to me on Valentine's Day,' I said.

Justine and Louise made yuck noises behind my back. Peter put his hand up, trying valiantly to smile.

'So you two are little lovebirds, eh?' said Barney.

'What do you call two birds in love?' asked Basil Brush. 'Soppy! Boom boom!'

'I think they're very sweet,' said Barney. 'So who gave *you* this lovely locket, Peter?'

'It was my nan's,' Peter whispered. Two tears spilled down his cheeks.

'Oh, Peter, *don't* cry,' I said.

'I'm not crying, Tracy. I – I've just got hayfever,' Peter snuffled.

I looked at him. My heart gave such a thump I had to clutch my chest. What was the matter with me? Why were there tears in my own eyes? I was Tracy Beaker, tough as old boots. Why was I worrying so? The silly old locket wasn't worth anything.

I couldn't kid myself any more. The locket was worth the whole world to Peter – and he'd given it to me.

'I can't *do* this!' I wailed. 'I'm sorry, Barney. Please don't get mad at me. I know I'm wrecking your programme and I so want a karaoke machine but I *can't* swap the heart. It's all Peter's got left of his nan now. It's maybe not actually *real* gold but that doesn't matter, it's worth much more because it was so special to him and yet he gave it to me. So now I'm going to give it back to him. Here you are, Pete.' I took it off and handed it to him.

'Oh, Tracy! We wanted the karaoke machine!' said Justine-No-Heart-At-All-Littlewood.

'Well, maybe we can see if you can *win* a karaoke machine,' said Barney. 'We've got our three teams set up to brave the dreaded Gungulator. How about you guys challenging the winners? Just two of you. Let's see – Tracy and Justine!'

'But we can't be in a team *together*! We're deadly enemies.' I protested.

'There's no way I'm ever being part of a team with *Tracy*,' said Justine. 'I'll be in a team with Louise.'

'No, no, Peter and me will be a team!' I insisted.

'Count *me* out of any team. I'm not going in that green gunge!' said Adele in horror.

'I'll go, I'll go, I *love* green gunge,' Maxy shouted.

'Hey, hey, shh you lot. Do you want to give it a go or not?' said Barney. He grinned at me. He grinned at Justine. 'Go on, girls. Swallow your differences.'

I didn't want to let Barney down. I looked at Justine. She looked at me. We both swallowed. Then we nodded.

So we sat and watched the rest of the show. Peter nestled right up to me, the heart locket round his neck.

'You can have it back though, Tracy. It *is* yours,' he whispered.

'We'll share it, Pete, OK. Now be quiet, I need to watch this game to see how it works.'

213

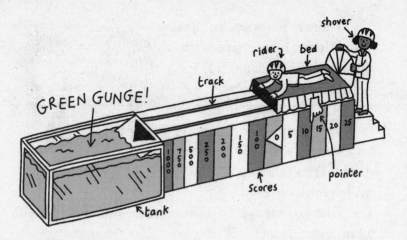

One kid got in a bed on a trolley. The other kid shoved the bed. They scored points the further it went. But if the shove was too hard then the bed went right off the scale and the kid tipped straight into the green slime.

We watched, we waited, we wondered . . . The Zebras team were defeated first. Then the Bees. So we had to beat the Tigers – with a final score of 100.

'We'll beat that easy-peasy,' I said to Justine.

'Of course we will,' she said.

'Good luck, Tracy!' said Peter.

'Good luck, Justine!' said Louise.

'Good luck both of you,' said Barney. 'Right, Tracy, you get on the bed first.' I got on the bed and Justine stood behind me.

'Watch what you're doing now, Justine. Don't be too feeble. Give a really firm push – but not *too* hard!'

'Oh, quit bossing me, Tracy Beaker,' Justine snapped and gave my bed a shove.

I shot forward.

I passed 50, then 100, 150 . . . I was slowing now, and I so needed to slow! I pulled hard on the end of the bed, trying to brake, but it was no use. I was edging further and further forward, past 200, past 250, past 500, oh no, past 750 and then . . .

SPLASH!

I screamed and swallowed a bucketful of icy-cold lime-green slime. I struggled to my feet, shaking my head, while the whole studio collapsed with laughter around me. *Right!* I'd show that Justine-Totally-Did-It-On-Purpose-Littlewood. In thirty seconds she'd be drenched in slime herself and see how *she* liked it.

I heaved myself out of the pool, snorting slime. Justine was practically wetting herself.

'Oh, help, it's a green slime sludge monster! No, wait a minute, it's Tracy Beaker!'

'You wait!' I said, as she clambered onto the bed and I took charge of the controls.

'Remember, Tracy, you want that karaoke set,' Barney called quickly. 'If Justine goes in the slime you'll lose your chance of winning one!'

My heart went . . . you've got it, thump thump thump! I sooo wanted to dump Justine in the green gunge the way she'd dumped me. But if I did then we'd lose our karaoke set and I sooo wanted that too. Not just for me. Peter and I could sing our duets . . .

I looked at Peter.

'Go for it, Tracy!' he yelled.

'Yeah, crack it, girl!' Adele shouted.

'Yes yes yes!' Maxy burbled.

'You can do it, Tracy,' said Mike.

216

'Do it for everyone, Tracy,' said Barney, giving me the thumbs-up sign.

I took a deep breath and gave Justine a sharp edgy shove that set her rolling. She went past 50, 100, 150, 200 . . . She was yelling like crazy now, ducking her head – but then she slowed to a dramatic halt, spot on the 250 sign. We'd beaten the others! Yay, we'd won!!!

'Well done, Tracy! You've won your karaoke machine for you and all your mates. I knew you could do it!' Barney shouted happily.

'I knew I could too!' I said. My heart went thumpety-thumpety-thump

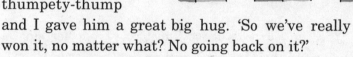

and I gave him a great big hug. 'So we've really won it, no matter what? No going back on it?'

'Yes, really,' said Barney.

'Great!' I said – and before Justine-Ever-Deadly-Enemy-Littlewood could get out of the bed I gave it one more shove. She shot straight into the green gunge. That wiped the grin off her face!

Join the FREE online

Jacqueline Wilson

FAN CLUB

You can learn all about Jacqueline from her monthly diary, her fan-mail replies and her tour blogs.

There's also loads to discuss on the message boards, you can customise your page, have your own online diary, put your picture into your favourite Jacqueline book cover and don't forget the competitions with incredible prizes!

Sign up today at
www.jacquelinewilson.co.uk

Jacqueline Wilson
The Dare Game
A Tracy Beaker Story

Illustrated by Nick Sharratt

*I'm Tracy Beaker, the Great Inventor of Extremely
Outrageous Dares – and I dare YOU not to say
this is the most brilliant story ever!*

I thought I was going to live happily ever after with Cam as
my foster-mum. Well, ha ha! It hasn't turned out like that.
Cam's so MEAN! She won't buy me designer clothes so all the
other kids at my new school laugh at me. No wonder I bunk
off and go to this special secret place. There are these two boys
I meet there, Alexander and Football. We play the Dare Game
– and I always win. I'm the greatest. I AM!

An all-time favourite Tracy Beaker story, now with an
extra-special new introduction by Jacqueline!

978 0 440 86758 6

Tracy Beaker is back . . . and she's just desperate for a role
in her school play. They're performing *A Christmas Carol* and
for one worrying moment, Tracy thinks she might not even get
to play one of the unnamed street urchins. But then she is
cast in the main role. Can she manage to act grumpy enough
to play Scrooge? Well, she does have a bit of help on that
front from Justine Pain-In-The-Bum Littlewood . . .

As Tracy prepares for her big moment, Cam is the
one helping her learn her lines. But all Tracy wants to
know is if her film-star mum will come to watch
her in her starring role.

978 0 440 86722 7

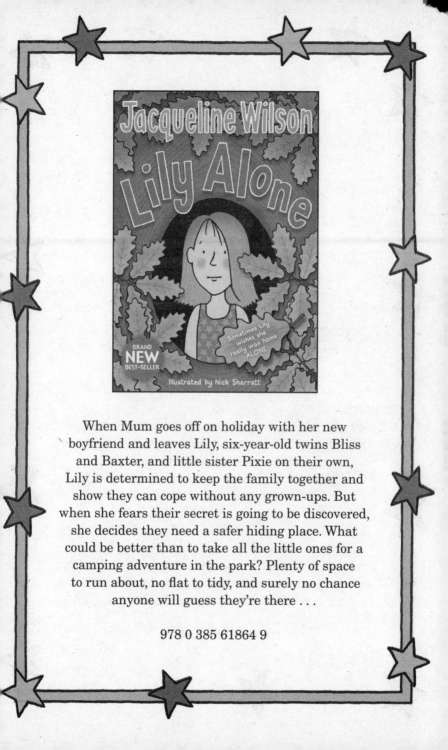

Jacqueline Wilson

Lily Alone

Sometimes Lily wishes she really was home ALONE

BRAND
NEW
BEST-SELLER

Illustrated by Nick Sharratt

When Mum goes off on holiday with her new
boyfriend and leaves Lily, six-year-old twins Bliss
and Baxter, and little sister Pixie on their own,
Lily is determined to keep the family together and
show they can cope without any grown-ups. But
when she fears their secret is going to be discovered,
she decides they need a safer hiding place. What
could be better than to take all the little ones for a
camping adventure in the park? Plenty of space
to run about, no flat to tidy, and surely no chance
anyone will guess they're there . . .

978 0 385 61864 9

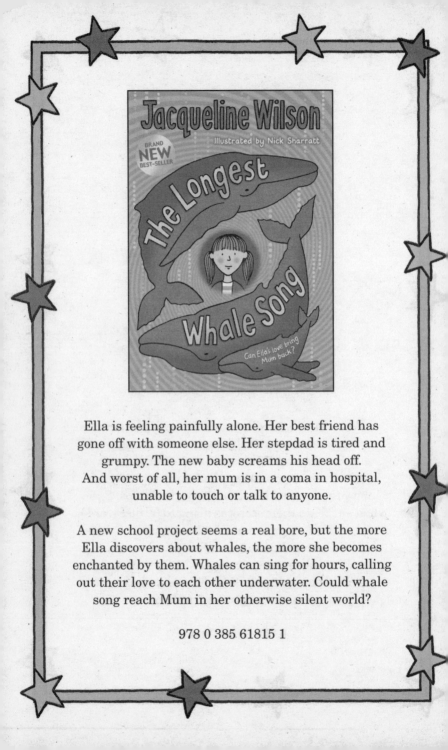

Ella is feeling painfully alone. Her best friend has
gone off with someone else. Her stepdad is tired and
grumpy. The new baby screams his head off.
And worst of all, her mum is in a coma in hospital,
unable to touch or talk to anyone.

A new school project seems a real bore, but the more
Ella discovers about whales, the more she becomes
enchanted by them. Whales can sing for hours, calling
out their love to each other underwater. Could whale
song reach Mum in her otherwise silent world?

978 0 385 61815 1

Sunset lives a glamorous celebrity lifestyle with her
rock-star dad and model mum – but yearns for
some peace and a real friend.

Destiny is the same age as Sunset but her life
couldn't be more different. She and her mum live on
the edge of a rundown estate, worrying about
money and illness.

When the two girls' paths cross, a surprising truth is
revealed and a very special connection is formed . . .

978 0 440 86834 7

There are oodles of incredible Jacqueline Wilson books to enjoy! Tick off the ones you have read, so you know which ones to look for next!

- ☐ THE DINOSAUR'S PACKED LUNCH
- ☐ THE MONSTER STORY-TELLER

- ☐ THE CAT MUMMY
- ☐ LIZZIE ZIPMOUTH
- ☐ SLEEPOVERS

- ☐ BAD GIRLS
- ☐ THE BED AND BREAKFAST STAR
- ☐ BEST FRIENDS
- ☐ BURIED ALIVE!
- ☐ CANDYFLOSS
- ☐ CLEAN BREAK
- ☐ CLIFFHANGER
- ☐ COOKIE
- ☐ THE DARE GAME
- ☐ THE DIAMOND GIRLS
- ☐ DOUBLE ACT
- ☐ GLUBBSLYME
- ☐ HETTY FEATHER
- ☐ THE ILLUSTRATED MUM
- ☐ JACKY DAYDREAM
- ☐ LITTLE DARLINGS

- ☐ LOLA ROSE
- ☐ THE LONGEST WHALE SONG
- ☐ THE LOTTIE PROJECT
- ☐ MIDNIGHT
- ☐ THE MUM-MINDER
- ☐ SECRETS
- ☐ STARRING TRACY BEAKER
- ☐ THE STORY OF TRACY BEAKER
- ☐ THE SUITCASE KID
- ☐ VICKY ANGEL
- ☐ THE WORRY WEBSITE

FOR OLDER READERS:
- ☐ DUSTBIN BABY
- ☐ GIRLS IN LOVE
- ☐ GIRLS IN TEARS
- ☐ GIRLS OUT LATE
- ☐ GIRLS UNDER PRESSURE
- ☐ KISS
- ☐ LOVE LESSONS
- ☐ MY SECRET DIARY
- ☐ MY SISTER JODIE